"ZEKE!" I scream, but . . .

I hear the first hollow, echoing sound of a fist and my heart falls from my chest. In an instant, Ezekiel and Marcus are into it, and something changes in Marcus's face. That easy-riding grin of his is gone, replaced by a look that's systematic and fierce, and I know he could kill Ezekiel if he wanted to. But I just watch as some of Marcus's homeboys start shouting at Ezekiel, too, looking like they're about to jump in. Almost like a reflex, Lavias goes running in and starts having it out with one of the guys. I wonder where my reflexes are, why I just stand there like I'm paralyzed or something. . . .

All of a sudden I hear some guy yelling at me in Spanish, and the next thing I know I'm taking him on, throwing punches like a maniac. I can't tell who's who anymore. . . .

"[Hewett] takes readers into the turbulent mind and soul of a 16-year-old African-American boy . . . and creates a thought-provoking novel that echoes today's headlines." —*School Library Journal*

OTHER PUFFIN BOOKS YOU MAY ENJOY

Fast Sam, Cool Clyde, and Stuff   Walter Dean Myers

Just Like Martin   Ossie Davis

Like Sisters on the Homefront   Rita Williams-Garcia

My Black Me   Arnold Adoff, editor

My Life with Martin Luther King, Jr.   Coretta Scott King

The Road to Memphis   Mildred D. Taylor

Teacup Full of Roses   Sharon Bell Mathis

The Young Landlords   Walter Dean Myers

Soulfire

Lorri Hewett

PUFFIN BOOKS

PUFFIN BOOKS
Published by the Penguin Group
Penguin Putnam Inc., 375 Hudson Street, New York, New York 10014, U.S.A.
Penguin Books Ltd, 27 Wrights Lane, London W8 5TZ, England
Penguin Books Australia Ltd, Ringwood, Victoria, Australia
Penguin Books Canada Ltd, 10 Alcorn Avenue, Toronto, Ontario, Canada M4V 3B2
Penguin Books (N.Z.) Ltd, 182-190 Wairau Road, Auckland 10, New Zealand

Penguin Books Ltd, Registered Offices: Harmondsworth, Middlesex, England

First published in the United States of America by Dutton Children's Books,
a division of Penguin Books USA Inc., 1996
Published in Puffin Books, 1998

10 9 8 7 6 5 4 3 2 1

LIBRARY OF CONGRESS CATALOGING-IN-PUBLICATION DATA
Hewett, Lorri.
Soulfire / Lorri Hewett.
    p. cm.
Summary: A rift develops in the closeness shared by Todd and Ezekiel,
two African-American cousins, when Ezekiel tries to single-handedly end
the problem of gang violence in his Denver neighborhood.
ISBN 0-14-038960-1 (pbk.)
[1. Cousins—Fiction. 2. Interpersonal relations—Fiction.
3. Afro-Americans—Fiction. 4. Denver (Colo.)—Fiction.]
I. Title.
PZ7.H4487So 1998 [Fic]—dc21 97-28235 CIP AC

Printed in the United States of America

To my parents,
Patricia and Russell Hewett

Soulfire

Chapter 1

YOU KNOW, IT'S FUNNY TO THINK HOW YOU CAN START looking at something and keep on looking at it until you forget you're even there. It's sort of like seeing a movie, where you get so involved in what happens on the screen that you stop existing for a while. The only thing that keeps me from forgetting myself now is the cold wind that blows over my sweaty skin, making me shiver a little. Otherwise, I just let my eyes travel over this old court on Twenty-sixth and Niagara, where I've been hanging out with my cousin Ezekiel and my partners Willy and Lavias ever since I can remember. Willy and I lost our game of two-on-two to Lavias and Ezekiel, but that doesn't really matter because Willy can't shoot worth a damn and it was just a little pickup game, anyway. Nothing to take too seriously. I lean up against the chain-link fence, sort of off to the side, while Lavias and Willy lie sprawled on the asphalt. Ezekiel's the only one on his feet, dribbling the ball around himself, cutting left and right like he's protecting the ball from five invisible defenders. But that's just how Ezekiel plays, like it's the final fifteen seconds in Game Seven of the NBA championships and it's up to him to win it all.

It's a nice, calm feeling, to sit here thinking about nothing in particular, watching the sun as it disappears behind the mountains. Not appreciating its beauty or any poetic crap like that, but just seeing the colors up in the sky, red and orange, like there's a fire going on up there. If I were alone, I'd wish I had a book with me, but I could never sit here reading on the court with the guys. I tried it once, and Lavias and Willy were all up in my face, making wise-ass remarks to try to distract me and stuff. And Ezekiel acts like reading's stupid, but I'll bet he just thinks that because they found out last year at school that he has some kind of comprehension problem.

I watch Ezekiel take a few running steps to the rim and jump up to jam the ball. He misses. The ball hits the backboard and bounces over to the fence.

"I don't think so!" cries Willy, stretching his long, skinny legs in front of him.

"I don't see you doing no better," Ezekiel retorts, running after the ball.

Willy grins. "I could make that shot with my eyes closed!"

Lavias laughs out loud. "Man, with them toothpick

legs you couldn't make that shot if the hoop came up and kicked you in your ass!"

"What're you talking?" Willy retorts.

Ezekiel ignores them. He picks up the ball, standing about where the three-point line would be, and shoots, the ball sailing through the rusty rim easily. Then he starts prancing around the court like it's Madison Square Garden or something instead of a worn-out-looking neighborhood court where the rims haven't seen nets since I don't know when and the faded gray asphalt crumbles under your feet.

"Oh, he thinks he's the man!" Willy shouts. Ezekiel turns around with a dirty look, and if I didn't know Ezekiel, I'd think he was really pissed off. He's got these heavy black eyebrows that knot together when he frowns. And his eyes are blacker than anyone's I've ever seen.

I just sit here, listening to the hollow, irregular thud when the ball hits the pavement, letting my eyes drift shut. Then I hear the whirring sound of an engine, and I open my eyes to see a dark blue Cabriolet stopping along the curb maybe a hundred yards from where we're all sitting, or anyway, close enough so that I can hear the engine cut off.

A tall girl with long legs steps out from the car, and the guys start looking at her because for one, she's real bright and has long hair. And two, she doesn't look like she's from the neighborhood. All the girls in this neighborhood, if they're dark or bright, are real designer-crazy, and all of them have Gucci or Fendi bags and stuff. But this girl just wears jeans and a plaid button-down shirt. She doesn't look stupid in plaid like most black folks do, and just from the way she walks I'll bet she doesn't give a damn about what people think of how she dresses, anyway. She walks toward us like she's got a purpose. Her eyes are on Ezekiel alone.

When Ezekiel sees her, a funny look crosses his face. He doesn't look all that crazy about seeing her, but I'm not surprised because girls bore him to death. "They never think about nothing important," he always says. As the girl steps closer, I realize I know her. She's in a class of mine at school, and her name's Leandrea something. Lavias looks her up and down like the ladies' man he is, but she stops in front of Ezekiel. She's almost a head shorter, but she looks right into his eyes, anyway. Ezekiel's eyebrows wrinkle a little. "What are you doing here?"

She looks at him for a moment. Up close she's even prettier than I thought, which is funny because most people don't look all that good close up. That's when you can see their acne scars and stuff. Her eyes are real light, blue or maybe even green, and her hair's brown and wavy, falling to her shoulders. She's not as bright as I first thought. She's actually more yellow, but you know she's definitely a sister because of her wide lips and broad cheekbones. "I was in the neighborhood."

Ezekiel shrugs indifferently. "What brings you to the hood?"

"I was driving by when I saw you . . ." Her voice sort of trails off as she looks at Ezekiel. Just looking at her, I can tell she's into him. A lot of girls think Ezekiel's good-looking. I guess he is. He's tall and he's got a nice build, even though he doesn't really work out or anything. He's a little on the yellow side, too. His mother was half Indian, so he's got sort of Indian features and reddish hair that he keeps shaved on the sides with a million tiny dreadlocks on top. But those black eyes of his keep him from being really good-looking, I think. He always looks like he's mad about something.

Ezekiel just looks at her suspiciously, his arms crossed over his chest. She stands there, shifting her weight, blowing hair out of her face, like she's embarrassed or something. So I think, what the hell, I can at least talk to the girl. It doesn't look like Ezekiel's all that interested, anyway.

"Whassup, Leandrea?" I say.

She looks away from Ezekiel and smiles a little, like she's glad someone's talking to her. "Todd Williams, right?" She's got a real pretty smile, I think.

"In person." I stand up and glance toward the curb. "That's a nice ride you got there."

"It's my mom's, but she lets me drive it," she says. "You're in my English class, right?"

"Yeah."

"You sit in the back of the room. That's why I haven't really spoken to you before." Her voice is low, without the squeaky giggliness of the girls that follow Lavias around at school and try to follow Ezekiel. And from the way she pronounces all of her words, I know she must live near white people or something.

I just nod like a fool, standing there like people do when they've run out of things to say. I'm about to ask her something stupid, like what she thinks about class, when Ezekiel says, "I'd get going if I were you. The hood ain't the safest place after dark."

Leandrea's face goes red, and I feel my own face getting warm, too. Ezekiel can be such an asshole sometimes. But before Leandrea can say anything else, Ezekiel squints, like he's trying to see something far away. I look around and see four guys coming toward us, walking alongside the concrete wall that separates this court from the one behind it. Three of them are tall and slim, wearing jeans and Raiders shirts with black bandannas tied around their heads. One of them's a little smaller. I recognize them all. My brother Marcus; two of his crew; and my cousin Tommy, the little one following behind. They come from the direction of Lancaster Oaks, a bunch of ugly gray rectangles that sits on the south side of this little court, which pretty much separates those projects from the houses where my friends and I live. When you think about it, it's sort of funny that the one thing country clubs and projects have in common is how they're named. Only a country club or a project would be called Lancaster Oaks. Maybe that's why everybody calls those projects The Club. Tommy follows after Marcus like a pet dog or something. Tommy's fourteen but he looks twelve, and I've never seen him hanging out with Marcus before. Marcus is seventeen, barely a year older than me, but standing in front of all of them, his shirt stretched across his chest, he looks older than the rest and definitely a lot older than Tommy. I start to feel uncomfortable real fast, wishing they'd walk by without talking to us, but then Ezekiel shouts, "Yo, Tommy!" in his loud voice, and they come walking over.

"Whassup?" Tommy asks as he slaps hands with Ezekiel.

Marcus grins when he sees me and the guys. "Whassup?"

"Nothing," I say in response, trying to sound cool but I'm not. I don't know exactly why I always feel weird around Marcus. He doesn't live at home, and I don't see him much. I don't know how you can describe someone like Marcus without sounding like some kind of social commentator or something. He is what he is; that's all I can say. Gang-banger, dopeman, high roller—whatever you want to call it—he wears jeans that sag halfway down his skinny ass and a Raiders cap cocked backward. Somehow or other, he ended up with slightly slanted, catlike eyes that make him look like he knows a lot more than other people, even though he acts ignorant.

Ezekiel glares at Tommy. "What're you doing hanging with them?"

Tommy stops grinning. I can tell he's trying to look tough, but he's at the age where he looks more like a girl than anything else. Pretty brown Mama-boy eyes and a big smile. His skin's brown and smooth, without all the zits I had two years ago. He stands there in saggy jeans and a black T-shirt that hangs off his twiggish arms because it's too loose.

Marcus looks Ezekiel up and down, like he's about to start laughing. "Hey, that ain't the way to be talking about family."

Ezekiel's frown deepens, but he ignores Marcus. "What're you doing messing with them, huh?" he barks at Tommy.

Tommy crosses his arms. "Whassup with you, man?"

"Don't pull that shit with me. You know what I'm talking about!"

Tommy narrows his eyes. "Man, you don't know shit."

"No, *you* don't know shit!" Ezekiel roars, pointing a finger in Tommy's face.

Marcus rubs his chin, sort of thoughtfully. "Hey, when was it up to you to pick the boy's friends?"

Ezekiel turns to look Marcus in the eye. "You ain't his friend. Shut up!"

Marcus throws up his hands. "And you are?"

Tommy looks from Ezekiel to Marcus, and I see a smug look in those big eyes of his. That little punk's never got this much attention from Marcus or Ezekiel in his life.

Ezekiel's fists clench and unclench. He turns to glare at Tommy. "These guys ain't shit. They can't do nothing for you."

Marcus takes a few steps toward Ezekiel, his smile broadening. Ezekiel turns to Marcus, and they stand face-to-face. Ezekiel wears his anger like a stamp on his ass, but Marcus's eyes remain completely empty. And it bugs me because I don't know what his next move's going to be.

Finally Marcus throws back his head and laughs out loud. "I get it, I get it. So you think you're a crusader and shit."

The others laugh with him, and Ezekiel stares back, his jaw rigid. I guess he can't really do anything else, even though he's making a fool of himself. I stand there, sort of mad, sort of embarrassed, hating that I have to be in the middle between Marcus and Ezekiel. That's why I can't really say anything. But then again, I don't know what I could say that wouldn't sound stupid. That's another thing about Marcus. The way he looks at you, like he honestly doesn't give a shit about you one way or another, just makes you look the fool, no matter how much you yell or scream. It's like yelling at a brick wall or something.

"C'mon, Zeke. Let's get outta here," Lavias says, but Ezekiel ignores him and shoves Marcus roughly in the chest. Marcus staggers a little, like he wasn't expecting it, but quick as anything, Marcus cuffs Ezekiel across the face, his fist making a nasty sound, and that's when Lavias and I grab Ezekiel's arms and drag him away.

"Let me go! Let me go, I can—" Ezekiel shouts, twisting and turning to let himself free. It takes everything in me to hold him back. Marcus's homeboys start laughing and talking shit, but Marcus continues to look at Ezekiel with that same intent expression. To tell you the truth, it scares me because I can't tell what he's thinking at all.

But all Marcus says is "Don't get into it with me."

Ezekiel shoves Lavias and me off and straightens himself up, glaring back at Marcus. There's something weird about the way his eyes dart from Marcus to Tommy. Yeah, he's pissed off, but there's something else there, too. Something I can't figure out.

Marcus points a finger at Ezekiel and nods, as if to emphasize what he just said. I stand there, uncomfortable as anything, until he and his homeboys turn to walk in another direction with Tommy running behind them.

"I'm not finished with you, Tommy!" Ezekiel shouts after them, but they don't turn around. We all keep watching them until they fade into the neighborhood, out of sight.

That's when I remember Leandrea. I glance around the court, but that dark blue Cabriolet is gone.

Chapter 2

EZEKIEL TURNS TO LOOK AT ALL OF US, STILL HUFFING and puffing like he's going to blow his top. There's an angry-looking slash mark on his cheek. Marcus has a ring with a diamond in it that must've cut his face.

Lavias throws Ezekiel a disgusted look, then shakes his head. "What was up with that?"

Ezekiel glares at all of us and I feel myself glaring back at him. I'm mad enough to take a swing myself. He should've known better than to start up with Marcus, especially over something stupid.

"What's all this about Tommy?" I demand.

Ezekiel doesn't answer.

"I don't get it," I go on. "Why do you all of a sudden give a shit what Tommy does?"

"I just do, that's all!" Ezekiel snaps.

I shake my head, thinking of all the times when we were kids, when Tommy would try to hang out with us and stuff and Ezekiel would tell him to leave us the hell alone. "You didn't give a shit yesterday—"

"Well, I do now!" Ezekiel's eyes are staring holes in the ground, and he looks like he's ready to kill somebody. I don't say anything else because I hate getting into it with him when he's pissed off. He just doesn't have any sense. It's like trying to reason with a two-year-old or something.

The sky's turning from red and orange to purple. "Let's get outta here," I mutter, and we all turn to head up the street.

"Hey, where'd that girl go?" Willy asks suddenly, kicking a rock that lies in his path.

"Back to the suburbs where she belongs," Ezekiel mutters.

"Yeah, like you know anything about the hood," Willy says.

Ezekiel's eyes flash. "I live here just like you do!"

Willy laughs. "Yeah, in a mansion."

Ezekiel scowls at the ground. "I don't live in no goddamn mansion."

Willy shrugs. "It's pretty damn close."

"Damn, that girl was fly!" Lavias exclaims. "Since Zeke ain't taking no interest—"

"Man, that all you think about?" Ezekiel sounds annoyed.

Lavias winks. "You know it!" At school the girls flock around him everywhere he goes. The funny thing is that he isn't all that good-looking. He's big-boned and built like a linebacker, so maybe they like his body or something. But he's got this lazy left eye that makes him look like he's glaring at everybody. Still, he's got a way about him that makes the girls go crazy for him. More than anything, I guess he listens to what they have to say. Girls love it if you listen to all their stuff.

Ezekiel shakes his head. "I just can't be bothered, you know? I got other stuff to be thinking about, instead of some stupid girl who's all about dressing and gossiping and—"

"The girl just wanted to say hello, not like she wants you to marry her," I say. My voice sounds a lot more pissed off than I mean it to sound.

Ezekiel glares at me. "What, you like her or something?" He laughs. "Oh, yeah, the two of you could quote Shakespeare together, and all that other English honors shit—"

"Shut up," I mutter as they all start laughing. They start making cracks like "Ain't it study time?" and "Man, I gotta review my class notes. I got a test next month!" and other shit like that. I just ignore them. I hate when they get on me about school stuff.

Evening in my neighborhood is anything but quiet. Houses line the streets about an arm-span apart, and most of them've been there at least thirty years or so. Ever since I've been alive, I don't remember the neighborhood looking any different. All the houses have old-fashioned front stoops where moms and grandmas sit watching their little kids playing Gangster in the streets. We all used to play that when we were little. Nobody plays Cops'n'Robbers around here because nobody likes cops.

We all stop in front of Ezekiel's house. "You all coming in for a while?" Ezekiel asks.

Willy shakes his head. "Nah, I got some stuff to do."

"Yeah, I gotta go, too," Lavias says and grins. "I gotta be meeting somebody."

I slap Lavias's hand before he turns around to go.

Ezekiel turns to me. "What about you? You got stuff to do?"

"Nah, not really," I say, following him up the yard to the door.

Ezekiel lives in a big house. It's an old three-story Victorian that towers above all of the other houses on the street. His father and my uncle, the Reverend Earl Washington, is a prominent member of the community. He's the pastor of the largest African Methodist Episcopal church in Denver, plus he's friends with the mayor, a couple of senators, all kinds of important people. Reverend Washington can afford to live in a much better neighborhood, but he likes living here in Park Hill, where most of his congregation lives. I guess it looks good to say, observe; here's a strong black man who hasn't forgotten his roots, still here among his own instead of running off to the suburbs. Something like that.

Right when you walk into the house you know the reverend is big-time. First off, there're all these statues he's brought home from his many trips to Africa sitting on tables facing the door. Then there's a big framed picture of the reverend with Dr. Martin Luther King, Jr., hanging over the statues. The reverend's got this big old Afro because the picture was taken in the sixties. Any time people come over to the house they always stop to hem and haw over the picture for a while. But Ezekiel walks by without really looking at it. All he's ever said about it to me is that he thinks his dad looked stupid with the natural. I think so, too, but I would never say it out loud.

"That you, Zeke?" calls the reverend from the kitchen in his baritone voice.

"Yeah, it's me." Ezekiel heads down a hall to the kitchen and I follow after him. "Whassup, Rev?"

Reverend Washington sits at the kitchen table in front of this big Chinese take-out spread with Ezekiel's three brothers: Jeremiah, Zechariah, and Isaiah. They sit like they're just finishing the prayer, but they all look up as we walk in.

My uncle turns to grin at us. "Hey, Todd, what's going on?"

"Nothing, really," I say.

"How's your mom? She wasn't at Bible study yesterday."

I shrug. "I dunno. I guess she's been busy." I don't like talking to him very much. I mean, he's a nice guy, but I just can't relate. He's too big. I don't mean physically; he's not that much taller than me or Ezekiel, but there's just this power about him that keeps him from seeming real sometimes. He looks just like you'd expect some big-shot reverend to look. He's in great shape, has that "distinguished" gray hair and the square-jawed I'm-the-man looks he gave to all of his sons. If he didn't smile all the time, I think I'd be afraid of him. He's a man who doesn't take crap from anybody and it shows. Especially not from his kids. I've been over here sometimes when Ezekiel got yelled at so loud I could feel the hair on my arms rise. He's never hit Ezekiel, though. He doesn't have to. His voice has enough of a blow in it to make you feel as bad as if he had hit you.

The reverend's eyes grow wide when he sees his son. I look at Ezekiel and see that the cut on his cheek has already started to turn purple. But that angry expression in the reverend's eyes clouds over and he sighs, putting on that I'm-so-disappointed look instead. "What happened this time?"

His oldest brother, Isaiah, who's about twenty or so, looks annoyed. "Fighting again."

Ezekiel ignores him as we sit at the table. Jeremiah, the youngest, and Zechariah, the next youngest, look from their dad to Ezekiel, sort of amused, I guess. I don't like his brothers that much. They sort of lost their personalities after their mom died. Ezekiel went crazy, but the rest of them went blank. All three of them look so much alike now I can hardly tell who is who, and all of them are talking about going into the ministry like their dad. Even Jeremiah, and Jeremiah's only eleven. But Ezekiel just shrugs and grabs an egg roll from the table. "I'm all right."

The reverend sighs deeply and shakes his head. "When're you gonna learn to control that temper of yours, huh?"

Ezekiel keeps steady eyes on his father as he shoves the last of the egg roll into his mouth. "Look, it's no big deal."

"It *is* a big deal; don't you get it?" Isaiah says, folding his big hands on the table like the preacher he's studying to be. "You keep getting in fights, you're gonna end up like all these punks around here!"

Ezekiel rolls his eyes. I want to, too, but I don't.

"Don't roll your eyes like you don't know what he's talking about," says the reverend.

"I know what he's talking about, but what he's talking about don't apply to me," retorts Ezekiel.

Isaiah sighs and shakes his head.

The reverend turns his black eyes to me. "Todd, maybe you can tell us what happened this time."

Ezekiel shoots his dad a dirty look, then sticks his elbows on the table, looking bored. I hate getting in the middle between Ezekiel and his father. "Like Zeke said, it wasn't a big deal. We were hanging out with Tommy—"

The reverend looks at Ezekiel, surprised. "You got in a fight with Tommy?"

I start to get mad at myself for bringing this up. "No, I meant—" I stop for a minute, trying to think of the easiest way to explain things. "Marcus was there and he and Zeke had a—misunderstanding."

The reverend sits up taller. "Marcus? Lord have mercy."

"It was no big deal," I say again, but I don't think anyone's listening to me.

"All the pain that boy's caused your mother." The reverend gives me that reproachful look I know he means for Marcus, but it makes me feel bad anyway.

"Yeah, well, now Tommy's trying to be down with him and his partners, you know?" says Ezekiel, raising his voice.

"They were just hanging out—" I say, but then Ezekiel cuts me off.

"Didn't you say that shit won't stop till we start taking 'em back, one by one? You said that on Sunday! Now it's another one of your nephews!"

The reverend frowns. "Ezekiel, you know I don't like that language at the dinner table."

Ezekiel's eyes flash. "But can't you see it? Now it's your own family; what're you gonna do, huh?"

"C'mon, forget about it," I say.

But Ezekiel doesn't hear me. He points a finger at the reverend. "All that preaching you do and it ain't for shit!"

"Zeke!" shouts Isaiah.

The reverend is quiet for a moment before he speaks. "I don't know why you're being so hateful when all I'm trying to do is show some concern for you."

I want to get up and leave like you don't know what.

"I admire what you're trying to do for Tommy, I do," the reverend says. "But you don't get anywhere by fighting."

Ezekiel sighs noisily. "Don't give me that we-shall-overcome-turn-the-other-cheek crap."

The reverend stares down at his plate of lo mein, deep in thought. But then he looks up. "What if we set up a task force at church? Zeke, you could organize it, give it a snappy name, set up different kinds of programs. I can talk to some people over at Channel Seven for publicity." Then he looks at me in a way I wish he wouldn't. "And Todd, you could start a tutoring program, help the kids with their studies." He laughs, like he's found the answer. "How's that for a summer project?"

Ezekiel wrinkles his nose. "Oh, yeah, so we could get Marcus and Tommy and all them together and read Bible verses and pray. Oh yeah, that'll do a lot."

No one says anything, and the reverend hangs his head a little. I gulp, feeling bad. When the reverend looks up again, he seems genuinely sad. "What is it, huh? Is there something I'm not doing for you?"

Ezekiel just shoves another egg roll into his mouth, chewing loudly.

The reverend takes a deep breath. "You spend so much time with Todd. I don't see him so—so angry about everything like you are."

Ezekiel looks up sharply. "Yeah, you've always been mad that I'm not an Honor Society boy like Todd, right?"

I laugh nervously. "Man, Zeke, you're crazy."

"I don't think so," he mutters and gets up to leave the table.

His three brothers start throwing down their food like nothing happened at all, but the reverend just sits there. There's nothing worse than seeing a grown man sad.

He looks up at me slowly, but I wish he wouldn't. I already know what he's going to ask me. He doesn't even have to say it. But he does anyway. "Do you know what it is that's wrong with him? Do you know what it is that I'm not doing?"

Man, what can you say to that? I shovel my mouth full of food so I don't have to talk.

The reverend sighs. "Well, I'm glad to see that you aren't so irrational."

Yeah, good ol' rational Todd. It makes me kind of sick, thinking about how I must look to the reverend, like some kind of goody-goody or something. "I'll, uh, go see what's up with Zeke," I say, mainly as an excuse to leave the table.

"Tell him to put something on that cut," says the reverend.

I practically run up the long flight of stairs to Ezekiel's bedroom. The door's closed, but I can feel the bass from his stereo vibrating the door. I open the door and then close it behind me.

Ezekiel lies on his bed, his hand over his eyes.

"Yo, Zeke," I say, stepping over a pile of clothes to sit at his desk. Ezekiel's always been a slob. Piles of clothes, and the boy's got more clothes than anybody I know, CDs thrown everywhere, and then there's that sort of funky smell from keeping a messy room closed up all the time. His room's practically wallpapered with posters of the Black Panthers. Bobby Seale on one wall, Huey Newton on another, both standing there with badass looks on their faces, black berets cocked over their eyes. On the corner of the desk sits a small framed photo of Aunt Jessie, who died four years ago of some woman's disease or another. When she died, Ezekiel turned and rammed his head through a wall, even though they didn't get along that well. He's still got this jagged scar from it that goes all around his neck. Then he didn't talk for a week.

"What're you doing, Todd?" Ezekiel asks without moving.

"Just checking up on you, man."

"The rev sent you?" He sits up hunched over, his elbows on his knees.

I go to turn down his stereo because I can't hear him all that well.

"I knew he was gonna send you up here. He always wanted me to be more like you. Y'know, smart and everything."

"Don't give me that shit," I say, but I guess I don't sound sincere because he shoots a split-second glare at me anyway.

Ezekiel sighs. "Y'know, that's what eats me up. The man preaches every Sunday about all the shit going down in the neighborhood, saying we got to save all the ones who're messed up, and so I try to do that and he jumps all over me!"

I shrug. What can I say?

"And I hate the way he's always throwing Marcus

around like he's a lost lamb or something when I know he just thinks your brother's a damned liability. And him wanting me to start up a church group—man, that'd be the joke of the century." He shakes his head. "That's what messes me up about him, y'know? It's like, he can preach and holler on Sundays about everything wrong and he can volunteer to do all this shit but deep down, he's just another Tom."

"I don't know about that—"

"Yeah, he is. He's a Tom!" Ezekiel raises his voice. "He ain't never gonna do nothing to jeopardize his position in the community, so all the white people can say, now there's a Good Negro. He don't really give a shit about Tommy."

"But now you do?"

Ezekiel looks pissed off. "Whose side are you on, anyway?"

I throw up my hands. "All I'm saying is, what's Tommy to you? Before today you never said more'n three words to the kid."

"That's 'cause he's a punk."

"Man, I know he's a punk—"

"But the thing is, yeah, the kid's a punk, but just 'cause he's a punk he shouldn't end up dead. He's just trying to be a badass. I know it."

"But is it your business?"

Ezekiel nods firmly. "Yeah, it's my business. 'Cause

I'm sick of all the shit going down." He gasps a little and grimaces.

"You all right, man?" I say because he doesn't look too good at all.

"Yeah." He says this quickly and turns away from me. I start to feel uncomfortable so I start talking again.

"So whassup with you and that girl Leandrea?" I look at my hands so he doesn't think I'm fishing for information.

Ezekiel shrugs. "Ain't nothing between me and Leandrea."

"I dunno. I'd think there was something by the way she stopped to see you. She into you or something?"

"What do you think?" I don't know if I said this before, but Ezekiel can be one conceited sonofabitch. I guess it's good to know that he isn't interested. But then again, what difference does that really make? I could never come on to a girl like that. "You sure you okay? You look like shit again." I go over to stick my hand on his forehead. He's burning up. "Why didn't you say nothing about it, man?"

Ezekiel shrugs. "Nothing to say. All I need to do is sleep. Get out. I'm tired."

I back out of the room as he crawls under the covers in his clothes. He's shaking a little. Shivering. He's been getting these weird flash-fevers since January, when he went with his dad to Senegal. At first all the doctors thought he caught some third-world disease, like TB or something, but so far he's tested negative for everything. Since his wife died, the reverend leaves the country any time he can, taking his kids to all these random church conferences in Europe, West Africa, Indonesia, the Caribbean. I've seen the pictures. In all of them, the reverend, Jeremiah, Zechariah, and Isaiah are smiling and laughing while Ezekiel's always standing off to the side, not even faking it.

I stand there for a minute, watching Ezekiel lie there on his side, sort of doubled over. Then I walk down the stairs, shutting the front door quietly so the reverend doesn't hear me leave.

Chapter 3

IT'S SORT OF COLD OUT, BUT LIKE A FOOL I FORGOT MY coat, so I cross my arms over my chest and turn to walk up the street.

Tommy and another little punk come swaggering around the corner, like they're badasses or something. Kids are so stupid. I'm not all that much older than him or anything. But you would think there were ten years between us instead of just two.

"Whassup, cuz?" Tommy says and slaps my hand. I slap hands with his partner, too, even though I can't remember his name.

"Whassup with you?" I ask.

Tommy's eyes go narrow, and he looks like I pissed him off. "Man, you gonna start up that shit with me, too?"

"Nah, I just asked you a question," I say, beginning to wish I hadn't run into him.

His partner hits Tommy on the arm. "What's he talking about?" He looks even younger than Tommy does.

"My cousin Zeke, he got into it with Marcus, talking some shit like Marcus better stay away from me and shit." Tommy turns around to look at me. "What, he think he's my father or something?"

"I don't know," I say, because I honestly don't. "I guess he doesn't want to see you end up like Marcus or something."

Tommy throws up his hands. "Shit—"

"Hey, that's between you and Zeke," I say. I don't want to get in the middle of this. But I can't help but ask, "So you in or what?"

"Nah, not yet," Tommy said.

"Any day, man," says his partner and slaps his hand.

I just nod. They usually don't tell you when you're going to be initiated. They just grab you one day and damn near kill you, they beat you up so bad. I saw Marcus right after he was initiated. I never saw somebody beaten up so badly in my life. Both his eyes were black, plus his face was all lumpy and purple with bruises. He had these spongy-looking places on his face and chest where they'd hit him with something, like pipe. Come to think of it, Marcus wasn't much older than Tommy is now when he got beat like that. For a minute my mother's face comes to my head, that horrified-frightened-devastated-hurt look she had when she saw Marcus afterward, but I block that picture out real quick. And that fool kid doesn't even look scared. Well, not on the outside, anyway.

I mumble something to Tommy and we go off in opposite directions. It must be about eight o'clock or so because the sky's almost completely dark. Right now it feels like winter out here even though it's already April, and I feel like an even bigger idiot for forgetting my coat. But I'm always forgetting something. I don't know why. Maybe I always have too much on my mind. But I can't help thinking how stupid the whole thing is, Tommy being down with Marcus. Maybe I should care more about it, like Ezekiel, but I just can't. It's not like you don't see homeboys down with them every day. So what do you do: You stop and ask each one of them why? It'd eat me alive to think about that all the time. And then I remember how pissed off I get when I'm out somewhere and people start treating me like I'm down with all of that, too. Ezekiel was right about how all his father's preaching isn't going to change anything. So I have to wonder, was Ezekiel right when he tried to stand up to Marcus, knowing he could get his ass kicked, or worse? Hell if I know. But then I end up thinking about myself again. I can't think of anything I've ever stood up for.

I hear bass from a loud car stereo and look back to see a black Corvette inching along the curb, sort of following behind me. I turn to face forward and feel my feet speed up some, even though I have to make sure I look like nothing's up. The stupidest thing in the world to do is to start running, because then whoever it is will chase you, just for the fun of it. So I just keep walking with my eyes straight ahead, gulping every few steps to keep my walk steady, my breath going in and out with each step. I hate this shit. I really do. The car's moving slow enough and it's close enough so that anybody with half a brain could have a good clean shot at me.

But then I hear a loud "Whassup, Todd!" and I look over to see some of Marcus's homeboys hanging out the car window. I grin and wave, even though I'm mad enough to kick somebody's ass. The car speeds up the road, out of sight. I know they were just doing that to mess with me, but still, the shit freaks me out because you never know who it is in a car. And because of Marcus I always have to be careful. Sometimes people try to start up with me because of him, but that doesn't happen too much. I have to worry, though, because somebody's always getting shot. It's always somebody that somebody else knows that you know. You know, Tevin's cousin, Brian's brother, that sort of thing. Sometimes it's somebody you know, and then you just shake your head and say, "Damn." And when somebody dies, which happens a couple of times a year, well, you go to the funeral and watch people cry. Then you go home. If you're real unlucky and it's someone you know really well, like someone in your family, then maybe you cry, too, but you still just go home afterward.

I guess it's all a matter of perspective really, because Denver isn't South Central Los Angeles or anything like that. I mean, nobody sleeps in bathtubs to avoid stray bullets, or nobody I know, anyway. All I can say is that there are people you just don't mess with because everybody's got guns, and that's what you have to worry about more than anything. There're some crazy mothers out there who'll shoot you just to be doing it. I try not to think about it much because it's just a fact of life, you know? But that just brings me back to what I was thinking before. I mean, maybe everything'd be different if we all just stood up and took a risk, like Ezekiel did today. Then again, standing up to people doesn't mean crap if you get shot.

I've walked about a block past my house before I look up from the ground and see where I am. All that thinking really spaces me out in the head. I turn and run back to my house and up to the front door.

The bars on the windows make it look like a prison from the outside, especially when the lights are off. But most of the time the lights are on. Somebody's always coming or going.

I walk into the living room, where my oldest brother, Gerald, is staring at the TV. He must've just gotten off work because he's wearing a sport jacket and slacks. His shirt's unbuttoned almost halfway to the waist, and he sits on the edge of the sofa like it's a hardback chair or something. Ezekiel calls him The Stiff Without One. I call him that, too, but I don't say it to his face because he's likely to kick my ass.

"Whassup, Todd?" he says as I come in.

"Nothing." I go to the chair where I left my backpack earlier today.

"Work's a bitch." Gerald sighs. "Nobody's buying anything." Gerald works at a car dealership. I can't remember which one. Something Japanese, I think.

I look up and shrug because I didn't ask him how his day was or anything, even though he's looking at me like I did. "Too bad." I can't think of anything else to say.

"Yeah." Now Gerald leans back on the sofa, but he still looks awkward. "Shitty times. And I'm behind on my tuition payments for school. I gotta sell me a car by this weekend."

"Shitty times," I echo. That's true, though; it sucks to be working on commission. But Gerald makes a good salesman. He can bullshit with the best of them. He's nineteen but he looks older, which is why he got the job. Plus he's got that sort of bland Joe Handsome type of looks that high school cheerleaders go for. When he was in high school, he was the shit. Played basketball, got recruited by some crappy junior college that he goes to now. He was one of those guys who could date a white girl and nobody'd say anything. He still does. Date white girls, I mean.

I don't say anything else to him. I see a book I'm supposed to be reading at the bottom of my backpack and open it up so I don't have to talk to him. I don't like talking to him. He smiles too much. I don't know if I just hate it when black people smile like that or if I hate black people who smile like that. It reminds me of those old black-and-white movies with the grinning, tap-dancing maids and butlers.

My sister Kinesha comes running down the stairs, all dolled up in a frilly yellow dress. "It's my baby sister!" Gerald grins, opening his arms wide for her to jump into them. Kinesha hugs him and kisses his cheek.

"Toni got mad at me cuz she says I messed up her closet but I didn't!" She crosses her arms and pouts. "I just went in there to get something. It was already messed up!" She glances at me as if she just realized I was there. "Hi, Todd."

I sort of nod at her, but she isn't paying me any mind anyway.

Gerald laughs and tweaks her nose. "Well, you tell her I said leave my princess alone."

"I will!" she says, snuggling up to Gerald. She's nine but acts like she's about three. Gerald lets her, I guess.

He strokes her hair. "Listen, sweetheart, your big brother just got home from work and he's tired. Are you gonna go out and play or something?"

She nods, jumping down from his lap. "Are you gonna come tuck me in tonight?"

"You bet!" He grins at her as she runs out. I stare at my book, acting like I wasn't listening to them even though I was. It's sort of weird and sort of stupid, the way Gerald acts around Kinesha. It's weird in the sense that if I didn't know better, and if Gerald looked a few years older, I would swear he was her father or something. But it's sort of stupid at the same time, because Gerald comes off like he's the responsible Man About the House or something when all he does is sell cars and play basketball.

The door slams and Marcus stomps in. I look up and watch him cross the room to sit on the couch next to Gerald.

Neither one of them says anything because they don't really have anything to say to each other, but the air gets real thick between them. You can feel it. Marcus just sinks back into the couch and chills. Gerald stiffens up even more and the corners of his mouth go hard. The Stiff Without One. It's funny to watch them, because they look a lot alike. The three of us have the same father, so we all have these greenish eyes and dark skin, plus since I grew about five inches last year, we're all about the same height. Gerald's bulky, because he works out all the time, while Marcus is on the skinny side. Marcus'd be real good-looking if he'd gain some weight and stop doing all that mess, but I don't think he cares one way or another how he looks. And me? I'm more on the skinny side than Gerald but not so much as Marcus. I don't go around thinking much about the way I look. I'm not vain that way. Maybe I could be more of a ladies' man or whatever if I wanted to be, but that's not really in me. I guess I keep to myself too much, especially at school. Marcus is a senior in high school when he goes. I see him around at school every now and then, but I've never seen him open a book in my life. And Mom, well, she doesn't really know what to do about him, so she just lets him be. I don't even know what he's doing here really, because he doesn't stay here overnight all that much.

Canned laughter from the TV makes the only noise in the room, and the TV's glare gives both Marcus and Gerald ghostly gray appearances. Out of nowhere Marcus says, "Man, Zeke is full of shit."

I look up and see Marcus smirking. "What?"

Gerald looks up, too, like he's all of a sudden interested. "What'd Zeke do now?"

"I mean, the shit was funny when you think about it," Marcus goes on. "I didn't know he felt so much for Tommy. Almost broke my heart."

Gerald snorts. "What, he interfering in your criminal activity?" That's just like Gerald to say something like that. Marcus ignores him. Even though Marcus still grins, it bugs me because I never know what's up with him. In fact, I don't really know what he's capable of. To my knowledge he's never killed anybody, but I've seen him after he'd hurt people real bad, and he had that same smug I-don't-give-a-shit expression on his face he always wears. I really don't know how it is that he does not give a shit about stuff. I know some of it's all the crap he's into, but it's got to be more than that because I've seen homeboys get real mean when they're high. But Marcus, when he's high and when he's not, he's just this even flow of nothing.

I get up and go upstairs to my room because I don't like to be around him.

My room looks sort of bare, with dingy, yellowish walls. I don't have any posters up. I used to have some basketball posters. Typical stuff like Charles Barkley and Michael Jordan and Hakeem Olajuwon, but I took them down a few weeks ago. I guess I just got tired of looking at them. I really should put something up there, but I can't think of anybody famous who I'd really want to be looking at right now. Posters make people seem fake, anyway.

Gerald pokes his head in my door a few minutes after I've lain down on my bed with my book. He comes into my room and sits on the edge of my bed. "What happened between Marcus and Zeke?" he asks.

I shrug. "Nothing."

"What do you mean, nothing?"

"They just got into it a little bit, no big deal."

Gerald looks confused. "Marcus said something about Tommy. They got into it because of Tommy?"

"Tommy was hanging out with Marcus, and Zeke got pissed off," I say, getting a little pissed off myself. "That's it."

Gerald shakes his head, sort of the way people do when they've written somebody off. His look, which tells me that he thinks he's figured the whole thing out on his own without knowing any of the details, pisses me off even more.

"Did Officer Phillips or any of the others come?"

"No." I hadn't even thought of that. There're a couple of cops who hang out in our neighborhood all the time, so we all know who they are and stuff. To tell you the truth, I think they're all one big pain in the ass because they stop people for stupid crap and don't do a thing when you really need them. "I'm glad they didn't. You know how they act toward anybody who ain't in a suit."

Gerald shrugs. "I don't think it's what you wear; it's how you act."

I don't say anything.

"What are they supposed to do?" Gerald goes on.

"Ever think about it from their side? They're trying to protect the neighborhood from people like Marcus. How can they know who's on what side, huh?"

When I don't say anything, he sighs like he's a disappointed father or something. "All I know is that I'd hate to be a cop. I mean, what else could you do? If it looks like a punk and talks like a punk—"

"I've got to read this for tomorrow," I say, because I'm sick of hearing his voice.

Gerald looks interested. "So you still doing all right in school?"

I slam the book down on the bed and glare at him, wishing he'd get the point and leave.

Gerald throws up his hands. "Look, I just—" Then he lowers his hands and sighs. "I just get so worried, you know?"

I don't say anything and he puts his elbows on his knees, staring at the floor. "You don't know what it does to Mom to see Marcus this way. It's like I got all this weight on my shoulders, like I gotta keep everything from falling to pieces—"

"Nobody made you the man," I mutter.

Gerald looks up at me quickly. "What did you say?"

The frown on his face only pisses me off more. "I said nobody made you the man."

Gerald gets up in a huff. "I made myself the man!" he

snaps. "Somebody had to." He leaves, slamming the door behind him.

Once again, I open my book to read. Man, I'd never want to end up like Gerald. I know he really cares about stuff, but he always sounds so damn phony and condescending I can't stand listening to him. I cringe all over again, thinking about Ezekiel getting into it with Marcus and how I just had to stand there and watch. Maybe I should have said something to Marcus downstairs, stood up for Ezekiel or something, but I can't think of any way that I could have. Even if I tried, I couldn't be bullheaded like Ezekiel. But it seems weak to me to always be in the middle of stuff without taking a side one way or another. That's why it's so nice to not think sometimes. Sometimes I wish I was more like Marcus in that way, to be able to let stuff slide off my back like it's nothing instead of letting things get to me all the time.

Chapter 4

I WAKE UP A HALF HOUR EARLY BECAUSE MY TWO sisters are yelling in the bathroom. I can't get back to sleep on account of their howling, so I figure I might as well get up and knock their heads together, if I have to, to shut them up.

Toni and Kinesha argue over who used the last of the oil sheen or something like that. Toni towers over Kinesha, looking like she's about to slap the girl across the room. The bathroom is damp and steamy, and the sweet, greasy smell of oil conditioner hangs in the air.

"You all take your fight somewhere else," I mumble, searching for a clean towel in the heap on the floor. They keep yelling as I rummage through the damp towels. I find one that's reasonably dry, then turn to my sisters once more. "Both of you all, get out, 'fore I throw you out!" Girls under the age of fifteen should be locked up somewhere, I think. Or at least my sisters should be. They're always hollering and whining over stupid, insignificant stuff.

They sulk and stomp out of the bathroom and I proceed with my lukewarm shower. There's never any hot water in this house. Then I go to the mirror to run a hand along my jaw, seeing if I need to shave. I'm a little stubbly, but I figure I can go another day. I only have to shave about once a week or so. It's not that I'm underdeveloped or anything. I'm just not a hairy person. I read somewhere that black men are less hairy then white men anyway, and some of those white guys I see in gym class put the monkeys to shame. But aside from checking out my face for stubble and pimples (I only have one), I don't look at my face too much. I don't like looking at myself, because I can't help but see some of my father and some of Gerald in my reflection. And if I hate looking at them, how can I like looking at myself?

Next I brush the naps out of my hair. (It's getting sort of raggedy. I'll have to get Willy to give me a trim.) Then I throw on a pair of jeans, my number 12 Eagles jersey and my Nike Airs, and I go down the stairs to the kitchen to snag a little breakfast before Ezekiel comes to pick me up for school.

The kitchen's a mess. I brush some crumbs off the counter into the sink full of dishes I'm sure as hell not going to wash, then rummage through the fridge till I find some bread and orange juice. The Cheerios box on the counter's empty, so I figure toast'll have to do it.

Gerald's already sitting at the table when I sit down. I don't say anything to him. I just pick up the sports page after he's done with it.

"Yo, Todd, when're you gonna go see Dad?"

I keep my eyes focused downward so that he doesn't see the frown I know is on my face. I guess he hadn't heard a word I said last night. Figures.

"You need to go see him," Gerald continues, and I feel his eyes on me. "He keeps asking me about you."

"So?" I keep my eyes on the paper, trying to keep the edge out of my voice. That's why I can't stand Gerald. He never gets off that damned responsibility trip. Just because he carries his ass over to our father's house, he tries to make me feel guilty because I won't. And I don't think my father cares much one way or the other, really. The only thing I can remember Marcus ever saying about our father is "Dad ain't shit. Never has been, never will be." I'll agree with Marcus on that one. So I try to think about Dad as little as possible. Makes life simpler that way.

Out of nowhere, Marcus strides into the kitchen like he eats here every day. I didn't know he spent the night last night. He's wearing the same pants and black T-shirt he wore yesterday. He pours himself a glass of orange juice and joins us at the table. Nobody says anything to him, but Marcus just grins, like everything in the world amuses him. Everything gets quiet again until I hear footsteps and smell flowery perfume. My mom always wears flower perfume—too much of it, but it's a good way to know she's coming.

"Hi, boys!" she says brightly, but when she sees Marcus, the smile drops from her face. She clears her throat and puts on a pot of coffee, then joins us at the table. Just from her face I can tell she doesn't know whether to throw Marcus out or just pretend he isn't here.

"Hi, Mom," says Gerald, the only one who replies.

Mom smiles tightly, then picks up the front page, trying her damnedest not to look at Marcus. I guess she's decided to try ignoring him. I think what hurts her more than all the shit he's into is the fact that he just doesn't care about anything. And that makes her so sad, I can't stand looking at her. I mean, I don't know what it's like to be a mother or anything, but I think she cares about stuff too much. Then she tries to get back at people by acting like she doesn't, which makes her look stupid. I wonder if all mothers are like that. Every now and then I hear Mom praying for him, her voice low and strained. That really pisses me off, because it's not like her prayers are going to do anything to change Marcus. I don't know; it just sounds weak to me: Ignore him, then expect he'll change by getting down on your knees and saying a couple of prayers.

But it's not like she's a complete wimp or anything. My dad ran out on her after I was born; then Toni and Kinesha's dad divorced her to marry someone else, and another guy she was dating for a while ran off on her, too. I guess you can say she's beaten the odds; she had Gerald when she was seventeen, but she finished school and everything. She's only thirty-six, so she's still pretty young, and she works for an insurance company, so it's not like we're destitute or anything. Because she works so much, she doesn't spend much time at home, and I know she feels guilty about it. I hardly ever see her at all. But to see her face, with lines around her eyes that tell you how hard she works and gray hairs that tell you how much she worries, well, it just makes me feel bad.

A few minutes later Toni comes running down the stairs, all fixed up in this tiny miniskirt and tank top that shows off the tits she's already got, only fourteen and all. The girl's got on way too much makeup, and I can tell she must've spent an hour trying to put her hair up on her head like that. I don't know why girls are always trying to look older than they really are. Any guy with sense could tell she's a kid, even if she does have a body. She's got a kid's face and kid's eyes.

I hear Ezekiel laying on his horn, so the two of us go out to his car. Ezekiel has a blue Chevy Blazer, and Willy and Lavias are already sitting in the back. "Whassup?" I say as I climb in.

"Yo, Todd, I got this book report due tomorrow," Willy says, leaning forward all up in my face. "What if you do it for me, huh? I'll give you my one of my X-Mens."

"Get outta my face," I say, pushing his forehead away from me.

"Man, he don't want any of your damned comic books!" Lavias says.

In the rearview mirror I see Willy cross his arms. "He probably already read *Huckleberry Finn* anyway!"

I sit there wishing they'd change the subject.

"Is that the one with that stupid-ass slave who can't talk?" Ezekiel joins in. "Hell if I was gonna read that shit! Todd, you really read that?"

"Course he did!" Willy says.

I just shake my head, getting annoyed. I've known these guys as long as I've known me, but sometimes I feel like I'm a million miles away or something.

Ezekiel heads west toward the school and clicks on an Ice Cube CD with the remote. In the rearview mirror I see Lavias back there flirting with Toni, making her giggle and stuff. If I didn't know him better, I'd tell him to shut up. Not that I'm protective of her or anything, but it would sort of make me sick to see her with any of my partners.

Centennial High School's right in the middle of east Denver, and the place looks more like an old church than a school. It's been around forever, a huge mess of brown brick and stained glass. Both my mom and my dad went there. My grandma would have, too, but the school wasn't integrated back then, so she went somewhere else. But now this school's the most integrated place in Denver. Rich white kids, rich black kids who act white, poor white kids who act black, Vietnamese, Mexicans, gang-bangers, you name it. I head to my locker, saying "whassup" to a few people but basically keeping to myself because I don't really like to talk much in the mornings and I'm not really into the school scene anyway.

I'm standing at my locker looking for my English notes, which I'm afraid I left at home, when I hear some girl saying, "Hello again."

I look up and see Leandrea standing with her face not more than four inches from mine. Her hair's tied back behind her neck, and it's a little redder than I thought it was. Her hair's straight around the edges, so I know it's not processed. She's wearing jeans again, maybe even the same ones she had on yesterday, with a really pretty blue blouse that looks like silk or something. I have to blink a few times to keep myself from staring at her. "Whassup," I finally say, feeling like an asshole for taking so long to speak to her.

She looks sort of worried. "Was everything all right yesterday? With Ezekiel, I mean?"

"Huh? Oh, yeah," I say. "I didn't see you leave."

"Yeah, well." She shrugs, lowering her head a little. "I didn't want to be in the way, you know?"

I nod, not really knowing what to say.

"But everything was all right?" she says again.

"Yeah."

Leandrea smiles. "It's sort of funny, how we never really talked before yesterday."

"Yeah," I say and shut my locker. I feel myself getting a little nervous, but I don't know why. "So what were you doing in the hood last night?"

"Oh," Leandrea says, blushing a little. "I volunteer with the Girls' Club. I just go over there once a week and help the kids read. It's through National Honor Society. Aren't you in that? I mean, I've never seen you at the meetings, but I've heard your name."

I almost laugh out loud at that one. I got a letter last year telling me I got into Honor Society and I nearly flipped out. I got a big gold-edged certificate and everything. The guys got a real hoot out of that. I still haven't lived it down. I almost didn't tell my mom because I knew she'd do something stupid like put the certificate up on the refrigerator. "Nah, I'm too busy to be going to meetings."

She smiles again. "Are you walking to English?"

"Yeah."

"Have you seen Ezekiel this morning?"

I feel my chest rise a little, but I play it off. "Zeke? Yeah, he drives me to school."

"Are you guys really close?"

"Yeah, he's my cousin."

"I didn't know you guys were related. So, Reverend Washington, he's your uncle?"

"Yeah. How do you know the reverend?"

"I go to Zion AME."

"For real?" I've never seen her there before.

"Yeah. I go with my father." She looks casual in a way that tells me she's a lot more interested in Ezekiel than she wants to show. "He's a pretty amazing guy. Reverend Washington, I mean."

"How do you know Zeke, anyway?" I ask, trying to keep my voice casual, too.

"He's in my history class. He and my teacher are always at it."

"Yeah? Why?"

"He's always pointing out things about black history our teacher doesn't talk about. Mr. George gets really mad at him sometimes."

"Is he black or white?"

She's got a faraway look in her eyes. "White. But I can see why he gets mad. I mean, from his perspective, even though I think Ezekiel's right. It's just that he can be so—hateful sometimes, you get put on the defensive, anyway."

I shrug, and if I'm right she looks a little worried.

"I guess I shouldn't be saying that, since he's your cousin."

"You ain't saying nothing that ain't true."

She looks a little relieved. "Well, anyway, one day after class last week, after he and Mr. George got into it, I went up to him and asked him to tell me more about the Black Panthers. That's what he and Mr. George were arguing over. And it seemed like Ezekiel knew a lot about them and I don't, really. So I asked him."

"What'd he say?"

Now she looks disturbed. "I don't know; he seemed indifferent. I mean, he said yeah and all, but he didn't seem all that interested anymore. I don't know. He seems like a real up-and-down person to me. I try to be nice to him, but then he acts like I'm this big pain in the ass or something."

I don't really know what to say to that, so I just keep looking at her.

She laughs, giggles almost, so I know she's embarrassed. "Sorry. I can run my mouth a lot."

"I don't mind."

The nervousness goes away as she smiles back. It's too bad that we're finally standing in front of our classroom. We walk in and I take my seat at the back. She just says "I'll talk to you later," smiles one more time, then goes to sit in the front of the room.

All the other kids are talking and laughing, but I just sit there by myself. In most of my classes, besides gym, of course, I'm the only black guy in there. I hardly ever see Lavias during the day because he takes classes like Wood Shop. Willy's in my chemistry class, but he's always cutting up and stuff, so he doesn't do all that hot, grade-wise. And I think part of the reason why Ezekiel's so judgmental about school is that reading's tough on him. He's really good with numbers, but he has such an attitude about everything that I think he gets lousy grades on purpose. He always says that his teachers don't give a damn if he learns anything because he's black. I guess there's some truth to that. Even in my English class, my teacher looked at me suspiciously on the first day, like she was wondering if I was in the right place. But I don't want to come off like one of those "acceptable" black people, the way Gerald does. Gerald takes on that Black Man's Burden crap, trying to be all friendly to white people and stuff, so they don't think we're all a bunch of heathens. I'm sure as hell not going to be anybody's Good Negro. I look over at Leandrea and see her talking with the white kids, but there's still something sort of reserved and distant about her, like she knows she doesn't belong, either. It makes me feel good to see that. Sometimes it really feels like I'm the only one who goes through stuff like this.

Chapter 5

I'M STANDING AT MY LOCKER AFTER MY THIRD-PERIOD economics class when Leandrea comes running up to me. Right away I know something's wrong because her eyes are big and scared-looking.

"What's going on?" I ask, shutting my locker door.

It takes her a second to catch her breath, but the scared look doesn't leave her eyes. "It's Ezekiel," she says, her shoulders heaving. "After history class, I was walking out with him, and then these other guys walk by and Ezekiel gets mad and runs after them. He just snapped or something!"

"Wait a minute, what guys?" I say.

She takes a deep breath. "I think it was those guys from yesterday. Ezekiel said something like, let's take this outside."

"Aw, shit," I mumble. What the hell did Ezekiel think he was doing? "Where'd they go?"

"I don't know," she says quickly.

We hurry out of the building, which is easy because

it's the start of the first lunch period and there're no hall monitors around. Once we're outside the building, we cross the street to City Park. Marcus and all his crew hang out there, same with a lot of their rivals, so a lot of shit goes down there. My heart starts beating fast. I think of Ezekiel getting into it with Marcus last night. I know Marcus meant what he said when he told Ezekiel not to mess with him.

My eyes strain to look past all the goddamn trees and grass for Ezekiel or any of the guys or maybe even Tommy or Marcus. We slow down to a walk, and I keep looking around.

"You're acting like you know what's wrong," Leandrea says.

I take a deep breath as we walk further into the park.

"What's wrong?" Leandrea asks again, sounding more forceful this time.

"Zeke and I got this stupid cousin named Tommy and he's down with my brother and all his—"

"Who's your brother?"

"Aw, man." I get sort of nervous. "I don't have time to explain the whole thing."

Leandrea looks me in the eye. "He's in a gang?"

"You can say that."

She nods slowly.

"And Zeke's got it in his head that he's got to keep Tommy out of it. I'm afraid he's gonna get himself in deep. Listen." Something just came to me. This wasn't the place for a girl like her. "Can you do something for me?" I unhook a set of keys from my belt loop. "This key here's to Zeke's car. It's a blue Chevy Blazer, license tag says 'Zeke' on it, real simple. Could you get it from the student lot and drive it to the front of the park?"

She nods quickly. "Where exactly?"

"Right at the entrance. I'll meet you in front of there."

She turns around to leave, and I start half running further into the park.

Up ahead, near a cement wall covered with black and blue streaks, a group of punks in black stand in a circle, shouting about something. Before I know it, I'm running toward them and pushing my way through the circle. Ezekiel's in there; I know it.

"Let me go! Let me go!" I hear Ezekiel shouting. He's struggling with Willy and Lavias, who hold him by the arms and are trying to drag him away from a stupid little trash-talking punk in a black T-shirt. Ezekiel's got a trail of blood running from his nose and one of his eyes is purple, but he's struggling like a mad dog. He suddenly breaks free and knocks the guy to the ground, and the two of them start swinging fists again.

"C'mon, man!" shouts Lavias, but no one really hears him. My eyes meet Lavias's, and his face is all tensed up in a look that's more pissed off than anything. I try to break through the new crowd that forms in an instant around the fight. I shove aside one punk who's about my height and he shoves me back, trying to start up with me, I can tell. I do my best not to listen to his shit and turn around and take a swing at him. Willy and Lavias and I rush to Ezekiel, who's being knocked silly by two guys larger than he is. I get a blow to the jaw in the process.

On the ground, Tommy scoots away from the crowd, bright purple splotches on his face. He yells at the top of his lungs. "Shut up, Zeke, you stupid—"

"Stupid kid!" Lavias shouts and in one movement picks up Tommy by the collar and shakes him furiously. Tommy swings his fists helplessly, but Lavias, twice as big as Tommy, shakes him senseless. He throws Tommy aside like a rag doll. "Just get outta here, kid!"

"Whassup?" I hear a familiar voice over all the noise. The voice is loud enough to get everybody's attention, but it isn't a shout. It takes me just a moment to realize the voice belongs to Marcus, and I go numb inside. I run to grab Ezekiel under the armpits. Willy manages to grab him by the waist. I clench my teeth, and with all of my strength, I help Willy pull Ezekiel away.

Everyone falls silent, and everybody's eyes turn to Marcus, who's standing there with his arms crossed. A couple of guys from his crew stand with him. All the other guys sort of go quiet, and I look around to see that all of them here are wannabes. It showed in the way they fought. Guys like Marcus are cold and precise when they fight, not excitable and jumpy like these guys.

Marcus and his homeboys just look around at everybody, sort of blank-faced. Marcus's eyes stop on Ezekiel. Ezekiel shakes himself free from Willy and me, still huffing and puffing. I swallow a couple of times because my throat feels dry.

"What's the problem?" Marcus asks, grinning in a way that makes me wish we could all just disappear.

Ezekiel glares at Marcus. "Just trying to prove a point," he says, his voice loud.

"By getting your ass kicked?" Marcus says in a way that makes Ezekiel look like a fool.

"Think you can kick my ass?" Ezekiel looks like he wants to make a move on Marcus, and in a flash, Willy and I have his arms again.

Marcus laughs out loud and shakes his head. "Still don't get it, do you?"

Ezekiel starts struggling, and it takes everything in me to hold him back. Those burning eyes of his sweep over everybody. "And look at you, trying to act like you're all down when you're nothing but a bunch of wanna—"

I kick Ezekiel behind the knee to get him to shut up.

He winces a little, but he keeps struggling. All the little punks just laugh, but they keep their eyes on Marcus and his crew, like they're getting their direction from him. I watch Tommy get up off the ground where Lavias threw him and go slap hands with one of Marcus's crew.

That sends Ezekiel into a frenzy all over again, and he starts bucking and kicking. "What the hell you think you're doing, man?" Ezekiel shouts at Tommy. "Do I gotta kick some sense into you? Do I—"

"Let's just get outta here," Lavias mutters, but Ezekiel pays him no attention. I look over at Lavias staring at the ground. Willy shifts his eyes around, trying to look cool, but I know he's as scared shitless as I am. And then I think, what the hell am I scared of? Marcus is my brother, for Christ's sake!

Ezekiel's voice blasts my ears, and I'm starting to get even more pissed off. He's yelling in my face and his breath stinks. Some of the guys start yelling back, obviously looking for another fight. Ezekiel jams his heel into my shin and I wince, cussing under my breath. But it gives him enough time to wrench himself away from me and Willy.

Marcus comes over to stand right in front of Ezekiel. For a second they just stand there face-to-face, like they did last night. My muscles tense, as I expect Marcus to cuff him or something, but he doesn't. Marcus just stands there looking at Ezekiel. Ezekiel glares back, but if I'm not mistaken, I see something else in his eyes, that same something I saw yesterday. I take my eyes off of Ezekiel long enough to look around at everybody else. The other guys are all staring at Marcus, too, sort of in awe. I know at that minute, if Marcus said "jump," they all would. Zeke has to see that, too, doesn't he? Is that why his mouth is twisted into that weird line and his eyes burn with something besides anger? Is he just plain old jealous?

Marcus doesn't say anything. He makes a gun with his finger and thumb, and, in a weirdly graceful way, slowly brings it to Ezekiel's temple. "Pow," he says, and if he's joking or not, I don't know. All I know is that I want to get the hell out of here.

"You stupid—" Ezekiel breaks, screaming, and tries to run toward Marcus; and this time it takes me, Willy, and Lavias to hold him back. Marcus just laughs as the others start shouting back.

"Ease down, man, ease down!" Lavias shouts as we pull him away.

"Where's Tommy?" Ezekiel shouts. "I gotta knock that kid upside the head! I gotta—"

"We gotta get him outta here," mutters Willy. That's when I see the Blazer crawling along the curb and Leandrea in the driver's seat.

"Where's Tommy?" Ezekiel continues to shout.

Lavias grabs both of Ezekiel's shoulders and yells right up in his face. "What're you doing? What the hell you think you're doing? You're gonna get yourself killed for a stupid kid." He sounds so angry for a moment I think he's going to lose it. But Willy shouts, "Let's go! Let's go!" and he and I shove Ezekiel and Lavias into the car. We jump in after them and the car pulls away from the curb, away from the park, away from it all.

Chapter 6

I TAKE A DEEP BREATH AND SIGH, THEN LET MY HEAD vibrate against the car window. Willy sits in the front seat, not moving, the back of his head so still you would think he was a statue. Lavias and Ezekiel sit in the back next to me, silent and stony-faced. Leandrea drives the car, her eyes fixed forward as she heads south. My jaw throbs where I was hit, pulsing with its own rhythm. I wince when I reach up to touch it. Ezekiel's a mess. Both eyes bruised, nose bloody, lip cut. Finally he gives all of us a sweeping glare. "I didn't need to be rescued!"

"What the hell were you doing, anyway?" I snap at him.

Ezekiel shrugs. "Some wannabes wanted to give Tommy his own little initiation before he goes in. Stupid shit."

"So what the hell you got to do with it? Playing superhero or something?"

Ezekiel looks pissed off. "I was talking to Tommy, trying to put some sense into him, when all those mothers show up and start messing with my program. Just self-defense, man. That's all."

I sit up straight and sigh. "And Marcus? What the hell are you thinking? You think that just 'cause he's your cousin he won't mess with you?"

Ezekiel looks defiant. "Naw, I don't think that. But see, I ain't afraid of Marcus."

Now Lavias shakes his head, looking disgusted. "You're gonna get yourself killed trying to look like a badass."

"I can take care of myself," Ezekiel mutters.

"It sure don't look like it," Lavias exclaims.

Ezekiel throws himself back against the seat. "I'm just sick of it all."

"Sick of what?" Lavias is yelling again. "I'm sick of hauling your butt outta trouble every time you open your mouth; what the hell are you sick of?"

"Stupid kids getting mixed up with gang-banging," Ezekiel says. "I can't help it; it pisses me off! And it ain't cuz Tommy's my cousin or nothing. But if nobody helps him, he could end up dead, or like Marcus!"

I shake my head in disbelief. His mouth is a little tight at the corners, the only indication that he might be in pain, but he doesn't make any effort to wipe his face at all. His face has a little twinge of that green color from yesterday. I don't bother to ask him what it is because I know he won't tell me. There's just some shit you got to take, he'd say. Take like a man. Whatever. I start getting this weird feeling. Then I can't look at him anymore. That bloody face, green from whatever the hell's wrong with him, it just pisses me off. Because now I have to start thinking about myself, how I never do anything but let my mind get messed up about stuff while Ezekiel at least tries to go out and do something. And then I remember the way I was scared enough to piss my pants when Marcus showed up and now Ezekiel's sitting there saying he wasn't even scared.

"We gotta get outta here," Lavias says, sounding tired. "Give all this a chance to blow over. I don't know what's gonna happen with Tommy, but if you hang low for a while nobody'll mess with you."

"You don't gotta do nothing. I'm okay."

"You're not okay!" Lavias shouts. "Are you blind, man? Don't you see what you're getting messed up in? You're making the wrong enemies, man! What if they started shooting, huh? Or what if they decide to come looking for you?" He slams his fist against the door, then crosses his arms.

Ezekiel says nothing, and we all just sit there, in our own little pissed-off worlds.

Leandrea is the one who breaks the silence. I jump when she speaks because her voice is so soft. I guess I sort of forgot she was here. "We could go to Winter Park," she says. "My family has a condo up there."

Lavias raises his eyebrows. "Winter Park?"

She nods. "We'll have to stop at my house to get the keys."

"How long could we stay?" Lavias asks.

She shrugs. "As long as we want." She turns the car into Southridge, this upper-middle-class neighborhood south of town. All the houses are big, with foreign cars out in front. You know, the whole 2.5-kids-and-Fido type of spread. I could have figured. She doesn't really look rich, but she looks like she's got something. There are some black families who live here, but they don't have anything to do with anybody in my neighborhood, that's for sure. This neighborhood's so quiet. It's hard to believe we're only ten minutes from City Park and all the crap there.

Leandrea parks the car in her driveway and runs into her house. Ezekiel watches after her. "Where the hell'd she come from?"

Nobody answers him. Willy and Lavias look like they don't care and me, well, I don't know. It's strange, how right it seems to me for her to be here. I can't explain it.

Ezekiel sighs loudly, but in spite of his bruises, he's grinning a little. "She following me or some shit like that?"

"Just shut up," I mutter, wanting to add, no, she wouldn't follow a conceited ass like you, but I can't say that because I don't know for sure. Or maybe I do, and that's the problem.

Leandrea returns a few minutes later with a small duffel bag and a set of keys.

"What're you doing here, anyway?" Ezekiel says, eyeing her suspiciously.

Leandrea looks thoughtful as she starts the ignition. "I'm not sure. I was talking to Todd, then everything happened so quickly . . ." Her voice trails off.

I guess she doesn't want him to know that she was the one looking for him in the first place. Maybe she doesn't want to look like she's really into him or something.

Ezekiel doesn't say anything else.

"I suppose I'd better drive since I know where we're going," she says, turning around to face him. "Is that okay?"

He throws up his arms. "Whatever."

After that, the only sound in the car is Snoop's *Doggystyle* CD, which relaxes me a little because I start getting into the bass line and it gives me something else to think about.

Then the music switches off, and I look up to see Leandrea fiddling with the remote.

"Why're you messing with my music?" Ezekiel demands. From the rearview mirror I can see a sort of grimace on Leandrea's face.

"Don't you have any other CDs? I don't want to listen to 'bitch this' and 'ho that' all the way up to Winter Park."

I grin when she says that, but I get embarrassed at the same time. I never think much about lyrics. I just listen to the music, you know? And all the girls I know like Snoop and Too Short and Dr. Dre as much as the guys. They just laugh at the lyrics.

She finds a Public Enemy CD on the changer and leaves it there. It's an old one, *Fear of a Black Planet.* She doesn't seem like the type who'd be into rap, but she seems to know the CD. So I sit there and watch her mouth moving along with Chuck D on "Welcome to the Terrordome," even though she doesn't make a sound. And I feel a little better. At least I don't have to think about everything that just went down.

The sun is high over the mountains, about to begin its descent in front of us, as Leandrea drives into Winter Park. I stretch my legs in front of me and yawn. Lavias is asleep, slumped against the door, breathing heavy.

"We're here," Leandrea says loudly. Lavias sits up with a start. I stare out the window at all these white buildings with red roofs, surrounded by mountains and flowers. I almost feel like I'm in another country or something.

Willy closes his eyes and breathes deeply. "Man, I love the mountains!"

Leandrea smiles and parks the car in front of a high-rise condominium complex.

"Do you ski a lot?" I ask as she leads us up a flight of stairs.

"My parents do. But I'm not very good, so I don't come very much."

She opens the door onto a living room decorated with beige furniture and pink scatter pillows, looking like something out of a home-decorating magazine. One of those fancy chess games with metal pieces sits on a little end table in the corner. A large bay window overlooks snow-covered mountains to the west.

We all wander inside and sit on the couches. Ezekiel pushes the pillows to the floor, looking bored. Willy looks around the place with the same look I know I've got on my face. That out-of-my-territory look. Nobody says anything for a minute or two.

Finally, Lavias speaks. "I wanna get it, Zeke. I wanna know why you're acting the way you are." He leans forward with his elbows on his knees, staring at Ezekiel.

Ezekiel doesn't say anything.

Lavias persists. "What the hell is it?"

"You know what's up. I gotta keep Tommy—"

"Stop all this shit about Tommy. I wanna know what's up!" Lavias says, looking pissed off. "Yeah,

Tommy's your cuz and all, but I know you don't give that much of a shit about him. I know you don't."

"What the hell do you know?"

"That you're full of shit."

Ezekiel throws him a look that makes me think that if Lavias wasn't sitting across the room from him, Ezekiel would have taken a swing at him. Lavias glares back. He doesn't give a shit about Ezekiel's tough act; I know it. Lavias weighs about forty pounds more than Ezekiel anyway, so it'd be easy to figure out who'd win that one.

"I mean, don't you ever get sick of it all?" Ezekiel's already-loud voice gets even louder. "Not just the gang-banging and stuff, but how we all be stabbing each other in the back and shit? We don't even need the peckerwoods to do it for us 'cause we do it ourselves! Don't that piss you off?"

"It pisses everybody off. So what?" Lavias says.

Ezekiel's not about to be calmed down. He's practically shouting. "Somebody's gotta do something, you know? Who's gonna stand up and be a man? Where're all the men, huh? I don't see any. They're either too busy licking Peckerwood's boots or sitting around doing nothing. Todd, what's your pop done? What's he done?"

"Aw, man, shut up!" I'm surprised at how loud I yell that.

"What, you protecting him? You trying to deny that he hasn't done shit? I mean—"

I look at those black eyes, wide to the point he almost looks crazy. For one second I feel like I hate him for throwing my dad in my face like that. "You don't shut up and we'll go at it now." That's all I say.

Ezekiel takes a deep breath, but he doesn't apologize. He's never apologized for anything in his life. "All I'm trying to say is that I don't know any black men who aren't afraid to be men. Really be men, you know? And stand up for themselves."

Lavias still looks like he doesn't buy it. "So what does Tommy got to do with being a man?"

"Did you see Marcus today? See the way he had all them punks dancing out of his hand? Man, all he woulda had to do was say 'take him out' and he woulda just stood there watching while they all tore me apart." Ezekiel sits up a little and there's something fierce in his eyes. "Why the hell should Marcus have that kind of power when he's nothing but a low-life punk? What kind of shit's that? So I figure, somebody's gotta turn things around, you know? Take the power away from him. And only a real man can do it, not some Praying Tom like the reverend or a lowlife like Uncle Gerald."

My anger's like a ball of fire in the back of my throat that I can't swallow down.

Ezekiel sits up a little taller. "And since nobody

else'll stand up, I guess I have to do it. I have to be the man."

Lavias laughs out loud. "And who the hell gave you permission?"

"Nobody!" Ezekiel says hotly. "I don't need no permission from nobody. I'm gonna go in there and take Tommy back."

I look over at Willy and see him staring at a wall, sort of blank-faced, like he's not really listening. Then I look at Leandrea and see her pretty face shining into Ezekiel's, like, I don't know, like she wants him to drink it up. Her face, I mean. I look at Ezekiel as he looks at all of us, his eyes skipping Leandrea entirely. I'll bet he forgot she's here. I wonder if she sees that, too. I hope she does.

"So you keep Tommy out. Then what?" Lavias says.

"I start with Tommy," Ezekiel says. "And then with the next wannabe punk I see and the next."

"So when do you become a man?" Lavias says sarcastically.

"You just don't get it." Ezekiel shakes his head. "You see, one of these days, when people start looking back, they're gonna say, 'Zeke Washington? Man, he was the shit.' Like Huey Newton, you know? They're gonna say, 'Look at what that guy did. Look at how he turned things around. He was a real black man.' "

"Uppity sonofabitch," Lavias mutters and turns away.

Man, I just want to erase all this and go home. Lavias is never like this. I've never seen him mad for more than five minutes at a time. But from the look on his face I would almost think he hated Ezekiel. Really hated him.

Before I know it, I'm up on my feet and heading toward the bathroom. I don't know, I'm sick of looking at everybody. I take a piss even though I don't really have to. Then I stand there a minute or two, staring at the toilet before I flush it and go to the sink to wash my hands. This whole thing sucks. And what sucks most is that I keep hearing what Ezekiel said about being a man and snatching the power. I remember how torn up I was last night, wondering if he was doing the right thing by trying to stand up to Marcus. What a waste of time that was. I think of how Ezekiel looked today standing there in front of Marcus, and I want to throw up. What a crock of shit. He just wants what Marcus has. It was branded right across that conceited ass of his. He wants people to jump when he says jump. He wants the goddamned glory. I squeeze my face with my hands, wishing I could squeeze all this crap out of my head and everything could go back to the way it was yesterday, when we all sat out there on the court before Marcus showed up. I wish I could stop everything from changing the way it is right now, completely out of my control. My head aches.

And then, somewhere in my aching head I think,

yeah, Ezekiel may be crazy, and maybe he isn't totally genuine about wanting to keep Tommy away from Marcus, but at least he could stand there face-to-face with Marcus and say he wasn't afraid. And if he meant anything in his ranting and raving, I know he meant that. I look at my reflection in the mirror, see the bruise at the corner of my mouth, and try to make the most badass-looking face I can. But I still look like a damned kid. I don't look like a man at all.

On my way out, I almost bump into Willy, who I guess is waiting to use the bathroom. I'm about to walk by him without saying anything when his voice stops me.

"Zeke's my man and everything, but if he talked about my pop like that, I woulda knocked him out," he says. He doesn't even look mad. He looks like his usual happy Jiminy Cricket self. But I know he means every word he said. "I woulda killed him," he says, closing the bathroom door behind him.

Chapter 7

BACK IN THE LIVING ROOM, THE OTHERS ARE LOUNGING around, doing nothing. I sit down on the floor, clenching my hands into fists for no reason.

Soon Willy comes back and breaks into a wide grin as he claps his hands together. "Got anything to eat around here?"

For some reason, his grin, big and crazy-looking, now makes me feel better. I feel myself grin, too, and this great big tense thing leaves the room. I know that sounds like some hokey Mary Poppins crap, but I can't explain it any better.

Leandrea stands up. "I'll order pizza. Sausage okay?"

"Just plain cheese for me," Ezekiel tells her. She nods and leaves the room.

Lavias raises his eyebrows a bit, getting that gleam in his lazy eye that shows he's interested. "So she's stuck with us up here?"

Ezekiel laughs out loud. "Man, you might as well say what you're thinking."

Lavias cops this innocent look; then he laughs, too. "I just said she was something. She must have a liking for you, anyway. She's been sitting here looking at you the whole time."

Ezekiel shrugs like it's nothing, and the muscles in my neck get stiff. I take a deep breath and try to look like nothing's up. But nobody seems to be paying me attention anyway. "That girl is fly—" he says.

"Man, fly ain't the word." Lavias shakes his head. "That girl is exquisite!"

"Exquisite?" Willy exclaims. "What, you been studying a dictionary or something?"

"Didn't know your vocabulary was more'n one-syllable words!" Ezekiel joins in.

"Aw, shut up," Lavias says, but he laughs, too.

"Exquisite," Ezekiel repeats. "I like that."

"I don't," says Willy. "Makes me think of china dolls and shit. And she ain't no china doll."

"Word." Lavias laughs. "Man, I'll bet you could show her some of that black power—"

"Aw, shut up!" I say, yell really, before I know it.

Ezekiel looks at me, surprised. "Whassup with you?"

"Just shut up," I mutter, staring at the ground. They don't say any more about it. I really surprise myself sometimes. I don't know why that made me so mad. I mean, we all talk about girls like that. Black power, well, it doesn't take a genius to figure out that one. It's not like we're serious about it or anything, it's just talk. But I don't want to hear that about Leandrea. I just don't.

Leandrea comes back and sits in a chair in the corner. Lavias and Ezekiel and Willy start talking about college basketball, but I sit there looking at Leandrea out of the corner of my eye. She doesn't say anything. She just stares into space, like she's not really here. I wonder if she knows we were talking about her. Something about her makes me think that she does. But it's not like she's all pretend indignant, like girls get when they know you've been talking about them.

The pizza comes a little while later; and Lavias, Willy, and Ezekiel pounce on it. Leandrea gets up and leaves the room, and for some reason, I follow her.

I find her sitting by the window in one of the bedrooms. She stares out at the mountains, a wistful look on her face. She doesn't see me come in.

I go to sit beside her. "Whassup?"

Leandrea turns to me. "This is my favorite part of the day, when the sun's beginning to set."

"Yeah?"

"Especially up here in the mountains. It seems as if the sun's going down over that next hill there." She laughs, but her laugh doesn't sound happy. In fact, there's something sad about the way she sits there.

"When I was little, I used to think if I climbed over that mountain there I'd be able to touch the sun." She chuckles. "I was a stupid kid, huh."

"Nah."

Her shoulders shrug slightly. "So you're not hungry either?"

I shake my head. I don't know why I'm not hungry, because I haven't eaten since breakfast.

"This is all so strange, how I ended up here with you guys."

"It's funny how some things turn out." I wish I could think of a way to talk to her without sounding like an idiot.

She leans her head against the glass, not saying anything else.

I start getting nervous, so I turn to look at the room. It's sort of small, but it's got that same home-decorating-magazine look that the living room has. The bed's got a flowery bedspread on it with one of those ruffly things at the bottom. There're a few landscape paintings on the wall. It doesn't look anything like I'd imagine someone's bedroom would look. It looks impersonal, like a nice hotel room or something. "This your room?"

"Yeah."

"It's kind of—" I don't really know what to say.

Leandrea smiles a little. "My mom decorated it. She wants it nice like this because Dad lets his business partners use the condo and stuff."

"It's nice—" I say, but I don't sound all that sincere.

"I think it looks stupid," Leandrea says. "I'm almost afraid to touch anything, like I'm going to mess it up. But it's not like I come here all that much, so I guess I shouldn't care."

I don't say anything.

"This is the first time I've brought people up here," she says.

"Really?"

"I'm not supposed to. When I got my driver's license, that was the first thing Dad said to me. He said, 'You're not going to party with your friends up at the condo.' "

"So you're gonna get in trouble?"

Leandrea's still looking out the window. "Probably."

I get a little uncomfortable. "We can clean the place up, make it look like we weren't here—"

She crosses her arms over her chest. "I don't think I care."

I sit there not knowing what to say.

"I'll bet Ezekiel's a real hard person to get close to," she says suddenly.

I turn away from her real fast. I don't want her to see my expression. You knew, man, I tell myself over and over. C'mon, you knew. But I feel like shit anyway.

"He's so headstrong, you know?"

"He's really into himself." I sound kind of harsh when I say that.

Leandrea sighs. "I can tell. I don't know, really. It's not like he's all that nice of a guy, but there's something going on underneath his skin, you know?"

I shrug.

"I'll bet you know, since you're his cousin and all and the two of you look really close."

"I dunno," I say. I definitely don't feel close to him right now. In fact, I don't think I've ever felt so far away from him.

"And whatever it is that's eating him up, I bet I could understand." She looks at me, raising her voice a little. "Even the stuff about wanting to be a man."

"You a shrink or something?" This sounds a lot meaner than I want it to.

But she just laughs, like she didn't hear it. "What I mean is that for some reason, I feel like Ezekiel and I have a lot in common. I know what it's like to be mad all the time about everything."

"Yeah?" I ask, surprised.

Her eyes cloud over a bit, like she's pulling back into her own shell or whatever it is that people pull back into. She turns to look out the window, sitting perfectly still. I sit there watching her, feeling something weird twisting at my insides. The light from the sun catches the red highlights of her hair and turns her skin all golden. I feel empty inside. I want to ask her what it is that makes her feel mad all the time, but I don't know what to say to her. I don't know how to let her know that she could talk to me and I'd really listen in a way that Ezekiel never would. I guess there's nothing I can say. So I get up and go back to the living room, leaving her alone.

The guys are lying on the floor around the pizza boxes, contented.

"Hey, where's what's-her-name?" asks Ezekiel.

"Leandrea?" I sit down with them and pick up a slice of cold sausage. "I guess she wants to be by herself for a while."

Ezekiel shrugs and the three of them start talking about something or another. I can't even pretend to listen. I sit off to the side by myself. It's weird, how you can be surrounded by people and still feel like you're all by yourself. I don't think I've ever felt this alone, even around the guys who know me better than anyone. Or maybe they don't know me all that well, after all. I think of Leandrea alone in the room, imagining her sitting there feeling alone the same way I am, and that weird twisting in my stomach starts all over again.

Leandrea returns a few minutes later, and I see the

wistful look has left her face. She looks as calm and re-served as she did before.

"So what were you doing in there by yourself?" Lavias asks as she sits down with us.

Leandrea shrugs. "Nothing, really."

Lavias grins, looking devilish. "Hey, do your folks keep any kind of stash around here?"

Leandrea looks a little taken aback, but then she shrugs.

"I could use a little relaxation, y'know?" Lavias says.

"I'll see what's here," Leandrea says and leaves the room.

Lavias looks at me. "And Todd, you could sure as hell use some relaxation. Sitting over there like you're about to explode or something."

I shake out my shoulders a little, realizing I must've had them all tensed up. And who knows what kind of look was on my face.

Leandrea comes back with a half-empty bottle of something that looks like vodka or gin. I can't see the label. She sits on the couch next to Ezekiel, who scoots over and looks at the bottle.

"Stoli?" Ezekiel says. "My dad keeps that shit in his liquor cabinet."

"This isn't exactly shit," Leandrea says.

"Stoli?" Willy asks. "What the hell's that?"

I don't say anything, but I'm wondering the same thing.

"Must be expensive," Lavias says, then puts his hands behind his head and leans back. "Give me a forty any day and I'm happy."

"A forty?" Leandrea asks.

Willy laughs. "You don't know what a forty is?"

Leandrea unscrews the bottle cap, looking a little embarrassed.

Willy keeps laughing. "Never heard of St. Ives? Colt 45? Old English?"

"You mean malt liquor?" Leandrea says.

Willy shakes his head. "Do I mean malt liquor. Man, that's funny!"

"Shouldn't be drinking that, anyway!" Ezekiel shoots. "The way those beer companies market that shit at black people—"

"Aw, you just say that 'cause you can drink stuff like Stoli," Lavias says. "Y'all can keep that. I'll take my forty."

Leandrea looks nervous. "I can go see if we have something else."

"Nah, don't listen to him," Willy says. "He's just talking out of his ass."

Leandrea unscrews the cap and brings the bottle to her mouth, taking a large swig.

"So the lady's a lush?" Lavias says and laughs.

She wipes the back of her mouth and hands the bottle to Ezekiel. "Lush?" she says, smiling. "I don't think so."

"I'll bet she's got all kinds of skeletons in her closet," Willy chimes in. "Looking all innocent."

Leandrea just laughs, but she doesn't say anything. When Ezekiel hands the bottle to me, I examine the label. That's when I figure out Stoli is some kind of good vodka. Then again, I wouldn't know a cheap vodka from an expensive one. It's all the same to me. I take a couple of quick swallows. I can't stand the taste at all, but I start to feel mellow real quick. I always get mellow whenever I sit around and drink with the guys. Willy gets silly, Lavias gets plain old crazy, and Ezekiel—well, it depends. You never know what's going to be up with Ezekiel. But as we pass the bottle around, I can't help but wonder about Leandrea, how she could feel comfortable sitting around drinking with a bunch of guys she doesn't know.

Leandrea turns to look Ezekiel in the eye. "Tell me about yourself."

Ezekiel laughs. "What?"

"Tell me about you."

He looks, for once, at a loss for words. His eyes dart around the room several times before meeting with Leandrea's. "What do you wanna know?"

Leandrea shrugs, and I can see in her eyes how

much she's into him. It almost makes me sick. "Well, what's it like to be the son of Reverend Washington?"

"Reverend Washington—" Ezekiel looks more thoughtful than he usually does. It must be the alcohol. "He's different at home than he is at church."

"What do you mean?" Leandrea asks.

"He gets pissed off at me, yells at me like any other dad, y'know?"

"Do you like him?"

"He's all right."

"What about your mom?"

"Dead." He cuts off the word sharply, like he's said all he'll say on the matter. Ezekiel never talks about his mother. "One thing I don't like about my dad is that he's so damn holy."

"Holy?"

"Holier than shit!" Willy interjects, laughing like a fool. He's such a lightweight.

"Yeah, holy." Ezekiel nods, sort of dramatically. "He always got God on his side, y'know? Sometimes when we fight, I think I'm fighting with God."

Leandrea laughs. "Really?"

Ezekiel takes another big gulp from the bottle. "Yeah. When I was little I used to hate God sometimes. 'Cause it seemed like God was more important than me."

"But God's the most important thing to a lot of people."

Ezekiel shrugs, lowering his eyes. "Yeah, but it's all so dumb, when you think about it. I mean, there ain't nothing wrong with believing in God. I just think He's kind of a jerk."

"Why?"

"'Cause anybody can have God on his side! The Bible-toting KKK people, they got God on their side, black folk got God on their side, everybody's got God on their side. So God must like messing with people's minds 'cause there ain't no way everybody can be right."

Nobody says anything.

Ezekiel goes on, raising his voice. "And I don't see no point in praying for forgiveness for stuff I'm not sorry I did. If God knows so much, then He knows people ain't sincere. And if He's so smart, then why don't He see that and stop forgiving people? Man, if I was God—"

"Man, if you was God you'd be sending everybody straight to hell," Lavias puts in.

"Nah, I just wouldn't mess with people's minds, that's all!" Ezekiel retorts. "Yeah, maybe I should be God. I'd make a good God."

"Shut up, you drunk fool!" Willy says.

"I ain't drunk; you're the one who's drunk!" Ezekiel shoots.

"Why don't you all shut up," I put in. I'm tired of hearing Ezekiel's voice, anyway.

"So you all get along okay?" Leandrea asks.

Ezekiel gets quiet for a minute. "The way I see it, your dad's supposed to be the guy you look up to more than anybody. 'Cause if you can't look up to him, then what, y'know?"

Something burns inside of me and I turn away real quick, feeling my face all screwed up. I could knock Ezekiel out for saying that, especially after what he said about my dad. When I turn around to look at him again, he's staring at the sofa. I'll bet he has no idea what he just said, what it meant. Then I get disgusted. That's just Zeke, self-centered through and through, alcohol or no alcohol. I look over at Leandrea and see her staring at the carpet in a weird way, like what Ezekiel just said bothered her, too.

But then she looks up at him again. "It just seems like Reverend Washington's such a strong man. I was wondering if you were alike in any way."

Ezekiel looks mad. "What, you trying to psychoanalyze me or something?"

Leandrea doesn't look fazed at all. "No. Just trying to figure you out so that when you're some great leader someday I can look back and say I knew you when."

I almost hate her for saying that. Somehow or another, she knew it was the right thing to say to Ezekiel because that suspicious look leaves his face and he grins at her.

"You're all right, you know that?" he says.

She grins back and I see his eyebrows raise a little, just enough to show he's noticing her. I want to yell, why the hell'd it take you so long? But of course, I don't. I never do.

Chapter 8

WE MUST'VE DRIFTED OFF TO SLEEP BECAUSE THE NEXT thing I know, I'm lying in a chair, my joints stiff as I don't know what, strong sunlight warming me from the east window. I sit up slowly and look around. Willy and Ezekiel sleep on opposite ends of the couch. Lavias snores away on the floor. Only Leandrea is awake, sitting on a chair and smiling at me. She's changed clothes, wearing a pair of jeans and a plain pink T-shirt. "Good morning," she says.

"Whassup?" I rub the gunk out of my eyes and then I wipe the back of my hand over my mouth in case I have drool marks or something. My mouth feels dry and cakey. At least I don't have a headache.

She stands up. "Are you hungry?"

I yawn and stretch. "Yeah—"

"We usually don't keep much food here, but I know we have some pancake mix." She walks toward the door. "We can go to the store to buy syrup and orange juice."

"All right." I get up slowly so I don't look too eager or anything.

I look around myself as we step outside, feeling like I've just stepped into a picture postcard or something. I've never seen a bluer sky in my life, and everywhere I look I see mountains covered with dark green trees. Leandrea shuts her eyes and lifts her face to the sun. "It's a beautiful morning."

"Yeah."

"I love it up here," Leandrea says. "It's too bad that I don't get many chances to come up here."

"Too busy?"

She nods.

"What do you do outside of school?"

She shrugs. "Nothing much."

I look her up and down, not really knowing what to think.

She turns to look me in the eye, which makes me jump a little because I wasn't expecting it. "Something wrong?"

"No, I was just wondering—" I don't exactly know what I'm trying to say to her. "I just haven't seen you around much."

"You were wondering what rock I crawled out from under?" She laughs a little. Then she puts her hands in her pockets and turns to face the road in front of us. "It's sort of funny, how we can go to a school like Centennial and still only hang out with a small group of people."

"Yeah."

We cross the street to a small supermarket, where a guy stands in the doorway, nodding to us as we walk in. "I guess you never saw me because I never really had any black friends," she says.

"So who'd you hang with?" I ask as we walk down an aisle.

Leandrea stops to pick up a bottle of syrup, Aunt Jemima grinning up at us from the label. She smirks. "That's a shame, isn't it? I mean, I grew up eating Aunt Jemima syrup on my pancakes, watching those dumb commercials with her talking to the little kids—"

"That's Mrs. Butterworth," I say, but I'm wondering why she didn't answer my question. I know she heard me.

She chuckles. "That's how I thought of black women for a while."

That throws me for a second. "For real?"

She nods, continuing to stare at the label. "One of my favorite movies used to be *Gone With the Wind*. It made the Old South seem so romantic. I used to dream about having a mammy to watch over me and dress me in frilly dresses as I waited for my gallant Southern gentleman to ride up on his horse—"

I don't respond.

Then she laughs and I notice she has a dimple in her left cheek. "Then one day I realized I was black. That sounds weird, doesn't it?"

"Yeah."

Leandrea lifts her eyes from the label and looks at me. "I mean, having a white mom made it easy to forget. And my dad's pretty color-struck, too. Anyway, I was watching *Gone With the Wind* one day about a year ago, and I thought to myself, Lee, why the hell would you want to live in the Old South?"

"So now you want to be down with all of us," I say, hoping she'll keep talking. We walk to the juice aisle, and she picks up a jug of orange juice.

She shakes her head. "It's not really that simple. I mean, you can't just go up to people and start hanging out with them." She pushes some hair out of her face. "I've hung out with the same people since kindergarten, kids from my neighborhood. My first boyfriend was Greg Loftgren. Do you know him?"

I shake my head, although I instantly get a mental picture of a blond baseball type in a Tommy Hilfiger shirt who I think was in one of my classes last year.

She continues. "And then, I don't know. So many of the black girls I've tried to get to know are just phony or they hate me because they think I'm after their boyfriends or something. And the guys, well, some of them think I'm easy because I used to date white guys and the rest think I'm stuck up."

I just stand there looking like a fool. I really don't know what to say.

"I'll bet the guys are wondering where we are," she says.

We go to pay for the food, then walk back out onto the street, neither of us talking. When we get to the door of her condo, Leandrea turns to me and smiles again. "I'm glad I got to know you, Todd."

"Yeah, same here," I say, meaning so much more than that.

All of the guys are awake when we walk in. "We was wondering where you all went!" Lavias says when he sees us. He's got circles under his eyes, but he looks all right. Willy has a funny look on his face, like he's got a sour stomach or something, while Ezekiel lies on the couch, looking half asleep.

"You don't look like you feel too good, man," I say to Willy.

Willy groans and lies back against the couch. "Shut up," he says, but I'm sort of suspicious because he's kind of a hypochondriac.

"Aw, had a little too much last night?" Lavias goes over to Willy and starts poking him. "How 'bout some nice greasy fried eggs and bacon for breakfast? How's that sound? With some corned beef hash—"

"Shut up and leave me alone, man!" Willy turns on his side and covers his face. Lavias just laughs and Leandrea and I laugh with him.

"How about pancakes?" Leandrea says. "Todd and I went to pick up some stuff for breakfast."

Lavias clasps his hands behind his head. "So what're you doing out here? Go make me some breakfast, girl!"

Leandrea crosses her arms and gives him a LOOK. That's the only way I can describe it. But she's still got a little smile at the corners of her mouth, like she knows he's just kidding.

Willy rolls over to look at Leandrea. "Uh-oh," he singsongs. "Homegirl's about to scratch your eyes out!" Even Ezekiel looks up, grinning a little.

Leandrea laughs. "Whoever helps me in the kitchen gets to eat."

Lavias jumps up and follows her into the kitchen, and I sit on the couch.

Ezekiel watches after her. "Lavias is trying to sink his teeth into her."

Willy laughs, and I have to figure he can't be feeling too bad. "Man, that is one smooth brother!"

Right then I hear female laughter, and the guys look at each other and grin. Even me, because I guess there's nothing really to fear from Lavias. I don't think he's her type.

I soon smell the buttery scent of pancakes and realize I'm hungry. I get up and walk into the kitchen. The guys follow me.

"Hey, y'all didn't help; y'all don't eat," Lavias says, bringing a plate of pancakes to the table. "You heard the lady."

"You all can set the table," Leandrea says, reaching up into a cupboard for some plates. I take them from her and put them on the table.

Ezekiel plants himself in a chair. "Y'know, this is some setup you got here." I look over at him, surprised that he's been so quiet. But I don't mistake a greenish tint in his face. He doesn't look hung over or anything like that. He's still sick, even though he won't show it.

"I'm glad you like it." She brings the juice to the table. "I can make more pancakes if this isn't enough."

We all sit at the table and begin to eat. Even Willy eats like there's nothing wrong with him, which makes me think there isn't.

"So." Willy looks at all of us. "What're we gonna do today?"

"Let's spend today up here!" exclaims Lavias after throwing down a huge stack of pancakes. "Check out the town, see the sights—"

"There isn't much to see," Leandrea says. "Just a bunch of overpriced clothing boutiques. I should be getting home, anyway."

"C'mon, we can stay up here for the day," Lavias pleads.

Leandrea looks at Ezekiel. "What do you think?" she asks him.

"I don't feel like it," Ezekiel says, sounding tired. He doesn't look good at all. He barely ate anything. Usually I'd be concerned, but to tell the truth, I don't really care. I guess I shouldn't be letting some girl change the way I think about him, but I can't help it.

"So just stay here, then, and we'll leave tonight," Lavias argues.

Ezekiel just shrugs. "I don't care."

Lavias grins at Leandrea. "So how about showing us around?"

"I think I'll stay here," Leandrea says. "I'm kind of tired."

"So who's gonna come with me?" whimpers Lavias.

"Me 'n' Todd'll go, so shut up!" Willy retorts.

I groan. The thought of Ezekiel and Leandrea alone together burns me up, but then I get even madder at myself for thinking that. I've never been a jealous type of person before, and it sort of scares me. And the boy is sick. So I say okay to Willy and Lavias, just to prove to myself that I haven't turned into a jealous son-ofabitch.

Lavias turns to Leandrea. "You sure you don't wanna give us a tour?"

She laughs. "I promise, there isn't much to see."

He hangs his head and sighs. "Oh, well."

We finish breakfast, and Willy asks if we should do the dishes. "No, it's okay," Leandrea replies. "Go watch TV or something."

Lavias grimaces. "Got any extra toothbrushes lying around?"

She shakes her head. "There's mouthwash in the bathroom."

He nods and heads toward the bathroom. I decide that's a good idea, and I follow him. He finds a container of Scope under the sink and takes a swig right from the bottle. He holds back his head and gargles, then spits it back into the sink. He hands me the bottle and I do the same.

When I return to the living room, Ezekiel's stretched out on the couch, his hands clasped over his stomach. I almost hate to admit it, but he really is a handsome guy. Those eyes of his put an edge on his good looks, but with his eyes closed, shoot. No wonder Leandrea's into him.

"Hey, Zeke!" I say softly. He doesn't answer. His chest expands and contracts lightly. The bruise over his left eye is already starting to fade, and I can't help but think how much he looks like Reverend Washington. In some ways they really are alike, even if Ezekiel claims they're so different. Both of them go after what they think is right; it's just that the reverend won't really piss anybody off the way Ezekiel does. You know, people always say that you can see a part of the father in the son. And even if Ezekiel's a lot more stubborn and pissed off at the world than his dad is, you can still see the reverend's presence, I guess you can say, in Ezekiel. I think of my own father, always sitting on his ass, and I wonder if anybody can see a piece of him in me. Let me tell you, it's a shitty thought.

Lavias comes bounding from the bathroom and joins us, slapping our shoulders. "Ready?"

"Yeah, hold on." I go to the kitchen, where Leandrea's wiping the table.

"You guys leaving?" she says.

"Yeah, but we won't be gone long."

"Okay. See you."

"Yeah."

As we walk outside, Lavias breathes deeply. "Man, this mountain air is something!"

"Don't be using it all up." Willy looks around. "Ain't this a cute little town."

"Just like one of them little places in Sweden!" exclaims Lavias.

"Don't you mean Switzerland, man?" I say.

He shrugs. "Sweden, Switzerland, what's the difference? Look, man, Benetton!" Lavias goes running toward the green sign on the corner of the street. He's always been really into fashion. Willy and I follow him into the store.

The store is small and cramped, its walls lined with all these trendy shirts and shorts. Lavias wheels from one display to another, but I stare at the floor, still thinking about Ezekiel and Reverend Washington and how they're always doing stuff. No wonder Leandrea's into Ezekiel. She said it herself—she likes the way he stands up for things, the way he tries to make himself a man. And then I wonder what I've ever stood up for. It seems like all I ever do is react to what Ezekiel does. An image of my father keeps popping into my head, and instead of blocking it out like I usually do, I let it stay there a while. Maybe I am like him; I don't know. Maybe that's why I never really say anything or take a stand on anything, outside my own head, that is.

"Hey, man, you with us?"

I look up to see Lavias parading around in a white shorts and shirt set. I grimace. "You can't wear nothing like that!"

Willy wrinkles his nose. "Man, you'd look like a pansy in some of that stuff."

"Nah, you just don't know nothing about styling," Lavias retorts. "No wonder you don't get the girls, dressed in them funeral clothes."

I laugh with him and even Willy chuckles, but he

crosses his arms. "Nah, you see, I look so good naturally I don't gotta be worrying about what I wear."

Lavias shakes his head. "Don't you wish!"

My eyes scan the store, and I see the employees, two blondes about our age, staring at us. I feel my face flush a little.

"Uh-oh!" Willy says, singsong. He must notice their expressions, too. "Something tells me we're being watched."

"We're being watched?" Lavias says, loudly enough for them to hear. He laughs and picks out another outfit. "Yeah, I get it. They ain't used to seeing niggers up here in the hills."

"Guess not!" Willy says cheerily, picking up a pair of shorts. "Hey, these ain't bad. Maybe I'll try 'em on!"

A dark-haired man steps out of a back room, his mustache curled downward. "What can I do for you boys?"

"We're just modeling your clothes, man," Lavias says and grins.

The man doesn't return the smile. He turns to walk over to the employees at the register, and they speak in low voices, occasionally looking our way. I don't even have to wonder what they're talking about.

We leave the store, and I can practically feel the sighs of relief from the employees as we walk out.

Lavias shakes his head. "Man, I'm glad Zeke wasn't with us."

I agree. I don't go shopping with Ezekiel anymore. One time he was accused of stealing at a Target store and refused to let the security guards search him. He caused such a commotion that the police were called, who promptly took him down to the station to question him. He fussed about it for weeks afterward.

When we get back to the condo, I don't see either Leandrea or Ezekiel. "Maybe they went somewhere," Lavias says, flopping on the couch. He starts eyeing the chessboard in the corner. "Hey, Will, remember how to play chess?"

"Remember? I killed you last time we played!" he says.

"But that was two years ago."

"You're on, man."

I ignore them, feeling my pulse speed up. I head down the hallway. Both of the bedroom doors are closed, and I don't hear anything from either one of them. I just stand there in front of them, my heart racing, afraid of opening either one of the doors and afraid to walk away. I picture Ezekiel in there with Leandrea, and the thought almost kills me.

Damn, Todd, it ain't like she's your girl, I have to say to myself. I know I don't have a right to feel jealous, but I do. And that just makes me feel sad. She likes Ezekiel, not me. Ezekiel's the hero to her, not me. But I open one of the doors a crack. There isn't anybody inside so I close it again, careful to be quiet.

I hear a sneeze come from the other bedroom, and my chest drops to my knees. They're in there. I should turn around right now, but I don't. I find myself opening that door, just like I did the other one. Maybe I'm into punishment or something. I don't know.

Leandrea and Ezekiel are in there on the bed. The first thing I see is that she's got all her clothes on. Ezekiel lies with his head in her lap. His shirt's off, but his jeans are on. He lies there without moving, his eyes closed. Leandrea's sponging his arms and chest with a washcloth. Something else rises in me when I see that. Ezekiel's sick, real sick, or he wouldn't be letting her do that. He just lies there. Leandrea's hand glides over his chest with the washcloth, and she looks at him like she cares so much about him. Something about the whole thing makes me sad. Makes me lonely. So I shut the door behind me and go back to the living room, where Lavias and Willy are in the middle of their chess game.

"Where's Zeke and Leandrea?" Lavias asks.

"Check!" shouts Willy.

"Aw, man, that ain't no check!" retorts Lavias.

"He's sick." That's the only thing I can get out of my mouth.

Leandrea comes out of the bedroom a few minutes

later. Her face is flushed, and she looks happy. Maybe she gets off on playing mother.

Willy and Lavias look up from their game.

"We should get going," Leandrea says. Ezekiel appears then but doesn't say anything. He's still a little pale, but he looks better.

"Yeah, let's get going," Lavias says.

"You just say that 'cause you're losing!" Willy says, then stands up. "Who's gonna drive?"

"Why don't you drive? I don't feel like it," Ezekiel says.

Leandrea locks the door behind us, and we all pile into Ezekiel's car. Leandrea sits in the backseat with Ezekiel, and I sit up front so I don't have to look at them. Every now and then, I look into the rearview mirror, and I see his arm around her. She leans against him and immediately shuts her eyes, her hair fanning all over his shoulder. Ezekiel lets her sleep there, against his shoulder. He stares out the window, looking almost like he doesn't know she's there. But seeing her there, looking so comfortable, it depresses me. So I shut my eyes and slide down on the seat.

Chapter 9

TWO HOURS LATER, WILLY DRIVES OFF I-70 ONTO Colorado Boulevard. "Hey, Leandrea," he says loudly. From the rearview mirror I see her fast asleep, all snuggled up next to Ezekiel. She sits up slowly and looks around, groggy-looking.

"Tell me where you live and I'll take you home," Willy tells her. She gives him directions to her house, still trying to smooth her messed-up hair. Ezekiel sits up now and rubs his eyes. He still looks sort of pale. Lavias stares out the window.

Willy parks the car in front of her house. "Here you go."

Leandrea stares at her house for a moment. But then she nods.

"Hey, thanks for letting us use your condo," Willy says.

She smiles slightly. "No problem." She looks at all of us like she doesn't know what to say. "I guess I'll see you all around—"

"Count on it," Lavias says and grins.

Leandrea climbs over Ezekiel to get out of the car, but then stands there for a moment. She looks at me and smiles a little. "Bye, Todd."

"See you 'round," I say, sounding as nonchalant as I can. I turn around quickly so I don't have to see her say good-bye to Ezekiel. But I see it anyway from the corner of my eye.

"I'll call you," he says to her. I can see his arms go around her.

"Damn, you all did get close!" Lavias exclaims as Willy drives out of the neighborhood.

Ezekiel chuckles a little. "She's all right."

I sit there hating the way he sounds so smug.

The houses get smaller and smaller and closer together the further Willy drives out of Southridge and into our neighborhood. It gets noisier, too, with little kids playing on the sidewalks and their grandmothers hollering at them to stay out of the street. All the loud-mouth girls stand on the corners in their tight shirts, their tits practically hanging out. I watch guys on the street whistling at them and stuff, and I wonder what Leandrea would do if she were here. Would she be pissed off if a guy whistled at her or would she just play it off, like it's no big deal? I don't know.

Willy drives to Ezekiel's house and parks the car out

in front. All four of us head up the front lawn to the door.

"You gonna be in a lotta trouble, man?" Lavias asks. "I know your pop ain't gonna be too happy."

Ezekiel shrugs. He uses his key to open the door, and we walk in to see Reverend Washington standing in the foyer, obviously waiting for us. And man, does he look like he's about to blow. His eyes narrow at Ezekiel.

Ezekiel stares back, not saying anything. I guess he knows better.

"Where have you been?" the reverend bellows.

"Out with the fellas," Ezekiel mumbles.

"All day and all night? You know, I even called the police looking for you! I thought something had happened to you!"

"Nothing happened," Ezekiel replies. "We're okay."

The reverend's eyes continue to flash angrily, and he raises his already loud voice even further. "And what was the reason for staying out all night without telling me where you were going? Haven't I raised you better than that? And Todd, your mother called me looking for you!"

Lavias, Willy, and I stare at each other uncomfortably.

Ezekiel says nothing. He looks directly into his father's eyes, his face expressionless. The reverend continues to yell, and the rest of us sneak out the door and sit on the front porch. We can still hear him from where we sit outside. Ezekiel is silent.

Lavias shakes his head. "Man, that reverend can yell something!"

Willy shrugs. "It just shows he cares. He's got a right to be worried, y'know?"

Lavias retorts, "Aw, man, you just say that 'cause you don't got to put up with it."

I don't miss the sort of weird expression that flickers over Willy's face. His dad got killed in a fight a year or so after he was born, and his mom has a new boyfriend almost every week. It doesn't take any brains to figure out why he's so silly all the time. If he wasn't, he'd probably be crazy.

We all say "later" and I head up the street to my house. Kinesha's playing in the yard with some of her friends. She looks up when she sees me. "Todd! Mom's been looking for you."

I shrug and go inside.

Gerald's lounging in the living room with a few of his old jock friends from high school. "Todd, you're back," he calls as I come in. "But really, don't come home on our account!"

I don't reply, heading for the kitchen. For some reason he gets up to follow me. I ignore him as I open the refrigerator.

"Mom's been worried sick about you, you know that?"

I don't reply. The fridge is practically empty. Mom must've forgotten to go shopping this week.

"But I guess you wouldn't care, would you." I can practically feel Gerald glaring, even though I've got my back to him. I see some ham and decide to make a sandwich.

Gerald sighs noisily. "No, I guess you don't."

"What's it to you?" I turn to the countertop and squirt mustard on a slice of bread.

"You were out with Zeke, right?" Gerald says. "What, he get in trouble again?"

I take my sandwich to the table, wishing he'd take his ass somewhere else. I don't want to talk about Ezekiel with him. I start eating so I don't have to talk.

Gerald clucks his tongue and shakes his head. "When's that stupid kid gonna learn?"

I don't reply. Instead I wolf down my sandwich and get up to make myself another one.

"Mom's worried about you," he says.

"What's that got to do with you?" I ask, getting pissed off because I know he's just trying to mess with me.

Gerald throws up his arms. "Don't you give a shit, man? What the hell's up with you?"

By the way he's ranting, you'd think I'd done something to him personally. "Forget you." I get up and take my sandwich up to my room, where I can eat in peace. At least he isn't fool enough to follow me.

No one's upstairs, so everything's quiet. I pull off my shirt, kick off my shoes, and lie down, surprised at how heavy my eyelids feel. I'm beginning to fall into semi-consciousness when my door opens.

"Todd!" It's my mother. "Where've you been?"

I sit up slowly and open my eyes to see her glaring down at me, her hands on her hips. "With the fellas."

"How could you go off like that and leave me worried sick? I called your father; he didn't know where you were! And Uncle Earl called looking for you. He even called the police—" My mother's voice sounds farther and farther away, and I fight to keep my eyelids open.

"Ma, I'm real tired—"

"Can't you give me one ounce of respect? I do so much for you and this is what I get?"

I just look at her, seeing the lines around her eyes, that worried-hurt look on her face. It really makes me sad. I guess she's gone through a lot because of Marcus and stuff, but I still hate feeling guilty all the time, like I have to make up for him or something. She continues to glare at me and I lower my eyes, wondering how I could tell her what was going on, but before I can say anything, she gets up and storms out of the room.

I lie back on my bed and stare at a wall, figuring I'll

talk to her later. I remember what I thought about up in Winter Park and decide that I'm going to go see my dad tomorrow. I'm going to see what kind of a man he is, if I can call him a man at all.

Chapter 10

MY MOTHER ISN'T SPEAKING TO ME SUNDAY MORNING.

She's sitting at the kitchen table reading the paper when I come downstairs. "Hi, Ma," I say as I sit down next to her.

She throws me a look, then sticks her head back into the paper. I sit there feeling like an asshole. But she's making such a big deal about not talking to me, all I can think is that it's her business if she chooses not to speak to me, so I just sit there for a while and then I go upstairs to shower.

Then I go see my father.

I hardly ever go to see him, but every time I do, he always slaps me on the back like it's only been a few days instead of a few months since I last saw him. Gerald sees him a lot, a couple of times a week, I think. But he still hasn't really done shit for Gerald, either. Dad used to bullshit me about why he left and all. He always said that he'd left because he was "still a boy" and he "needed to grow up." Then he'd scruff my head and say, "But your old man's a man now and he's gonna make it up to you." Yeah, right. I can't remember the last time Dad remembered my birthday, and for Christmas he'll throw together some half-assed present. This year I got a tie. He doesn't even know me well enough to know that I hardly ever wear ties.

I'm kind of surprised how diplomatic Mom is about the whole thing. She never talks about him, and if I bring him up, all she says is "Your father is who he is" and changes the subject.

My father lives a few blocks from my house with his girlfriend, Ann, and their two kids. He answers the door himself, a bathrobe tied around his gut. His hair is nappy and his face grisly, like he just woke up. But I still see traces of the good-looking guy he used to be in his face, especially in those hazel eyes my mother used to go crazy over. "Hey, Todd, what's going down? Long time no see!"

I shrug as he lets me in. The front room is a picture out of *Good Times* or something, cluttered with heavy black vinyl sofas and chairs, white stuffing peeking through the cracks. I sit on a sofa and my father sits in a chair across from me.

"So what brings you by so early? And where've you been off to? You've been a stranger to your old man!"

I shrug, staring at my hands in my lap. "I've been around."

"How's Gerald?"

"Fine."

He doesn't ask about Marcus, but he never does. "And what about you, son? You've been away so long; catch me up on what's going on!"

I don't reply. I catch my reflection in a wall mirror and see my face completely blank. I sit there trying to think if he's ever done anything. He's the king of "about to do something." About to start his own construction business, about to get married, about to come see his kids. Really, has the guy ever done anything to make anybody feel proud of him or even make him proud of himself? And then I wonder if I've ever really done anything. And nothing comes to me.

"C'mon, sixteen years old, I know you're running all over the place. Bet you're giving the old lady a lotta gray hair! That's what they say about the quiet ones, y'know?" He looks into my face. "Yeah, you're getting the Gerald Williams looks. I can see it. Gonna be a ladies' man just like your pop."

I just look at him. I wonder if it ever crosses his mind that he's never done shit for me. And I think, maybe if he at least looked guilty, or seemed nervous or something. maybe I could think he was sort of all right. But he just sits there, leaning back against the chair and smiling like we're best buddies.

"You okay?" He sounds concerned, but I know he's not.

I stare at the frayed carpet, unable to look at him any longer.

"You need anything? Some money or something?"

I look up real quick at that one. I can't remember the last time he offered me money. Usually he just complains about the construction market slump and how the union bosses never give him enough work. I look him right in the face. If I didn't know him better, I'd think he was sincere. And as much as I hate myself for thinking it, part of me wishes that I could pretend he was, the way Gerald does. For one second I want to start babbling off to him about all the shit that's on my mind, everything about Ezekiel that's bothering me, everything about Leandrea, and I want him to tell me I'm not crazy, that he used to feel confused about everything, too. I bite my lip really hard, hard enough to make myself wince. And then I taste blood in my mouth.

"You sure you're all right, son?" he asks again.

I stare at the floor. I'm kicking myself for coming to see him. I should have known I'd just get frustrated. My head feels like a rock, it's so tense. It's all I can do to open my mouth and say, "I'm fine."

"'Cause you know, if you need anything, you can

come to me," he says. "Things are going all right right now. I've been working a lot; me and Ann are talking about buying the house. A man's gotta plant some roots, you know."

I clear my throat. "So things are that good for you right now?"

"Not bad at all," Dad says.

"So you and Ann, you all're gonna get married?"

He's quiet for a moment or two. "Well, no, we haven't discussed that yet. Just between you and me, son—" He leans toward me a little. "She's gotta get her credit worked out. It really ain't a good idea to marry someone with bad credit because it'll just drag both of you down. That's what I tell Gerald, now that he's getting older."

"So what's wrong with Ann's credit?"

"Well, you saw that car out there," Dad says, sounding kind of proud. "I read up a lot before we bought it. All them auto guides say that the Saturn is the car of the future. And we got a great deal on the lease. It's just that Ann fell a little behind on the payments. Not much, but enough to have those idiots at the credit office calling here all hours of the day."

I hadn't paid any attention to any car, but I do remember Gerald telling me something about Dad getting a new car a couple months ago. "Isn't that your car, not Ann's?"

Dad nods. "Yeah, she bought it for me for Christmas. It's a gift."

Bullshit, I want to scream. I'll bet anything he talked Ann into buying that car, and now he leaves her with the bills?

"Now I'm getting settled, I wanna see more of you, kid," he says.

That makes me look up quickly, but I wish I hadn't because now Dad looks me in the eye and smiles at me.

"You know," he goes on, "I brag to all the guys at work that I got a genius for a son. I tell them my youngest boy's gonna leave his mark on the world."

I look away real fast, and to make things worse, I get this weird empty feeling. I frown at the floor until I get so pissed off that that feeling goes away.

But then, when I look up, I see that Proud Pop look on his face, the kind of look you see in the movies when the son scores a big touchdown and the dad's yelling his head off in the stands. I just—deflate, I guess you can say. It makes me sick to think that all he has to do is say something or look a certain way, and, instead of staying pissed off at him, I just feel mixed up instead. Maybe I should just shut him out completely, like Marcus does. I fight to keep my face blank. Damn if I'm going to let all this mixed-up shit inside me show. That's the least I can do, to keep it all to myself.

He claps his hands together. "Say, you hungry?"

I shake my head.

"Well, don't mind if I make myself some breakfast." He gets up and goes to the kitchen. I follow him and sit at the table while he goes to the stove. The kitchen's as messy as the rest of the house, with a sink full of dirty dishes. Dad starts frying some bacon and eggs. "You sure you ain't hungry? Looks like you could stand to put on some weight."

I don't say anything.

He comes to the table with a plate of steaming eggs and bacon. I watch him shovel the food into his mouth and gobble it down like it's his last meal on earth. "So how's your mother?" he asks with his mouth full.

"Fine."

"She dating anybody?"

"Nah. No time."

He cleans his plate and pushes out his chair. "Well, I'm planning on going to church this morning."

I nod, figuring I might as well catch a ride. "I'll go with you."

He grins. "Good. Let me get dressed. It's good seeing you, son. You gotta come see me more often."

"Like hell," I mutter.

"You say something?"

I shake my head. "Forget it." I sound really nasty. But

he doesn't seem to notice. He gets up to throw his dishes into the sink before heading upstairs.

Ann comes downstairs a few minutes later, dressed in a flowered skirt and jacket. She looks surprised to see me sitting in her kitchen. "Hi, Todd."

"Hi."

"What brings you by this morning?"

"To see my father. I think I'll head over to church with you all, too."

Ann looks me up and down. "Like that?"

I know what she's trying to say. I'm wearing jeans and a T-shirt.

She looks apologetic. "I mean, what you're wearing is fine for school, but—"

"God ain't into fashion."

She laughs nervously, her hands fluttering around her necklace. "No, it's just a matter of showing respect."

I shrug. I don't like her very much. Especially after what Dad just said about the car. I can't help thinking that part of the whole thing's her fault, too. I mean, she's the one stupid enough to let the guy walk all over her.

She doesn't say anything else to me. I'll bet she knows I don't like her. She gulps down a cup of coffee before going back upstairs. I sit in the kitchen until Dad and Ann come down, followed by two frilly-dressed, pig-tailed girls.

My father grins. "Ready to go?"

I nod and follow them out to the car. Sure, the car is nice. The interior's dark red and still has that new-car smell to it. It even has a CD player. I know they can't afford this thing. No wonder their house is such a shit-hole. The two girls fuss all the way to church, and one of them starts crying. Neither my father nor Ann pays them any attention.

Dad parks the car in the lot and Ann starts straightening up her clothes, like she's going on an interview or something. I get out of the car quickly and mumble something like "See you later." Then I go into the church by myself, filing in behind a bunch of old ladies decked out in pastel suits with matching hats.

If black people ever hold an impromptu fashion show, I think it should be held in a church. You can always tell when people are trying to outdress each other because every Sunday somebody's got on a new hat or a new dress, and all the old folks talk about it. I get several disapproving looks as I enter, but I don't care. To be honest, I'm not sure why I go to church, besides to see the guys. I sit by myself in the back-row pew so I can watch everybody.

Zion African Methodist Episcopal is an important church, the biggest and oldest AME church in the city.

And, like I said before, the reverend is IT. Whenever anyone wants an "African-American opinion," they go to the reverend.

My mom comes in, dressed up as usual, followed by a minidressed Toni, a dolled-up Kinesha, and a sharp-suited Gerald. Mom waves at me, so I guess she isn't mad at me anymore, but I don't follow them up to the third-row pew. Gerald gives me this look like he expects me to come sit with them, but I stay where I am. A little while later my dad and Ann come in with their two brats. I watch them go sit on the other side of the church, away from Mom.

Leandrea walks in with a tall blue-black man. She looks a little like him in the face, so I assume it's her dad. The girl looks sharp standing next to him. She's wearing this white jacket and skirt thing that's tight around the waist and shows off her legs, and her hair's piled up high on her head, showing off her long neck. From far away like that, she looks like the type of girl that me and the guys would always whistle at, joke about, but never think we could ever have a chance with. I start wondering why I haven't seen her here before, how I could have missed her. Maybe she just doesn't come to church very much. That same old ache from yesterday comes back when I see her. It's hard to believe I know her, seeing her like that. She looks untouchable. She doesn't see me, though. She follows her dad all the way across the church, and they sit in a middle-row pew sort of diagonal to me.

Tommy comes in with his mother, wearing a suit that's a little too big for him. It's funny; dressed up like that, he doesn't look like a punk at all. And from what I see, he seems to like church all right because every time I'm here he's here, too. He looks a lot like his mom. If she lost some weight, Aunt Lorraine could be really pretty. But in that white dress and with the white doily-thing on her head, she looks like an overweight nurse.

Willy comes in with his mother and his two sisters, wearing slacks and a white shirt. I grin and wave when I see him, but he goes to sit with his family up near the front. I like his family. His mother really doesn't care what he does, but she's always laughing and joking around, so you can't help but like her. His sisters are stupid. I mean, they're not much older than he is and they both have babies, so they're stupid in that way, but you can't help but like them, either.

Ezekiel and his brothers are seated in their customary front-row pew, looking all important in their black suits. The reverend always makes them wear suits on Sundays. I guess they have to make a good appearance or something.

The organist strikes up the processional, and all of the laypeople and associate ministers parade down the center aisle. Then, like a king or something, comes the reverend himself, followed by the choir. The church is only half full, but I know the pews will be filled by the time the reverend begins his sermon. Black people run on their own time.

I don't participate in the church service at all. I don't sing the hymns or repeat the responses, and I don't go to the altar for prayer. It's sort of the same thing I feel after I hang out with the guys on the court, like I'm in the audience of a movie or something and I'm not really a part of everything going on. Sometimes it surprises me, how much some people get into the service, like Aunt Lorraine. She's always shouting "Amen" and "Yes, Lord" and sometimes she even gets up and dances when the choir sings. I couldn't ever do anything like that.

I always listen to the sermon. I can't help it. Not only is the reverend loud as anything, but he has the kind of voice that punches you in the face. I look over at Leandrea. She's looking down, at her hands or the floor or something, but she looks like she's listening. Her dad leans back against the pew, his head tilted upward. Maybe he's asleep.

My eyes stop on Ezekiel far up in the front pew. I see only the back of his head, but from his motionless, upright position I can tell he's listening to everything his father's saying. I wish I could see his face.

I look up at the reverend and see him staring out into the congregation, actually looking people in the eye and stuff. I'm glad I'm sitting far enough away so that he can't look at me. He has a way of looking straight at people when he preaches, like he's preaching to that person alone. And believe me, there's no way not to feel guilty.

The reverend, what can you say about him? He's smart; he knows his shit. Maybe that's really what Ezekiel resents deep down. He says his father's a sell-out, a bootlicker, but what his father is more than anything is lofty. I look from the reverend over to where my dad's sitting with Ann and the kids. Dad seems to be listening. Every now and then he shouts "Amen," nodding his head up and down like he agrees with everything the reverend's saying. I look all around the congregation, from Leandrea's dad lying back against the pew, fast asleep, to my dad, acting like he's all holy, to the reverend himself, standing in front of everybody, holding everybody's attention. All I feel is an ache. At least Ezekiel's got someone who'll spend time with him and to try to teach him things, even if he doesn't agree with his dad on everything. But I can't really hate Ezekiel for not knowing what he's got, because I know what keeps the reverend from seeming real is that he's so far up there. For a second I imagine him sailing over the congregation right along with that big voice of his, just floating up near the ceiling. Because no matter how high anybody jumps, nobody can reach him. Definitely not me. Not even Ezekiel. Maybe I could feel sorry for Ezekiel if he wasn't such an asshole about things. But it's not even that, really. I guess it's Leandrea. Maybe I could feel sorry for him if Leandrea didn't like him. I get mad at myself for thinking that, because Ezekiel's blood and Leandrea's a girl, and girls shouldn't get in the way of blood. But I guess what keeps me from feeling sorry for him is that Ezekiel doesn't even know what he's got.

After the service I jostle my way outside. "Hey, Todd!" calls a low-pitched girl voice. My eyes scan the crowded front lawn until I see Leandrea waving at me.

"Hey yourself." I walk over to her. "Get in trouble yesterday?"

Leandrea groans. "Grounded for a month."

"Win some, lose some."

"I guess—"

"Where's your mom?"

Leandrea looks uncomfortable. "Oh, she doesn't like Zion."

"She go to a white church or something?" I ask.

"She doesn't really go to church. Did you get in trouble?"

"Nah. Yelled at mostly. Same with Zeke." I look back at her father, who's walking out to the parking lot. "So that's Pop."

Leandrea shrugs. "Yeah."

"What does he do?"

"He's an investment banker," she says, sounding sort of embarrassed.

Ezekiel walks up to us and claps me on the shoulder. "Yo, Todd, whassup?" He looks like he's feeling better, but he's still kind of pale.

"Nothing."

"Hi, Zeke." Leandrea smiles at him in a way that drives me half crazy.

Ezekiel hardly gives her a look. "Hey, whassup?" He turns back to me. "I ran into Tommy, man. I'm gonna try to talk some sense into him later on."

"I liked your dad's sermon," Leandrea says.

Ezekiel shrugs, looking indifferent. He turns the conversation back to Tommy and to me, but I'm hardly listening. I wonder why he's ignoring Leandrea. But she stands there listening to what he says to me, all this stuff about what he's going to say to Tommy.

"Lee, come on!" bellows her father from the parking lot.

Leandrea looks to the parking lot, where this Acura Legend sits out in the front. Figures. She looks back at us. "I have to go—"

Now Ezekiel has the gall to pay attention to her. He gives her this smug grin and says, "Wait a minute." He goes to put his arms around her and kisses her while I stand there feeling like an asshole. Then he lets go of her abruptly and turns back to me, like she was never even there.

"So you like her—" I say, watching her get into her dad's car.

He shrugs. "She's a nice piece."

That pisses me off so bad I want to haul off and punch him. "You shouldn't be talking about her like that!"

Ezekiel laughs. "What's your problem, man?"

I shake my head, really disgusted now. "You don't know shit."

Ezekiel throws up his arms. "Whassup with you? Did I say something?"

I frown. "I just don't wanna see you shit all over her."

He gives me a weird look. "I didn't know it'd upset you—"

"You don't get it," I mutter and start to walk away.

Ezekiel follows after me. "What's your problem? The last couple days you been acting like somebody dissed you hard or something."

I turn around and look at him. His eyebrows are knotted together and his eyes flash, but he doesn't look pissed off. He doesn't look all that concerned, either. In fact, he looks impatient. And all of a sudden, the whole thing seems useless. "Nothing," I say. "Just forget it." I turn around and start walking away.

"Hey, you gonna come over and hang out?" Ezekiel calls.

"I got stuff to do," I say without turning around. The church is about two miles from my house, so I walk home, glad to be by myself. I'm getting really sick of Ezekiel's shit.

Chapter 11

I KNOW SOMETHING'S UP MONDAY MORNING WHEN Lavias meets me at my locker after my English class. "Yo, Todd," he says in a sort of low voice.

When I turn to him, I see a worried look on his face. "Whassup?"

"It's Zeke."

"Shit," I mutter. What the hell else can I say?

"You went off to your class, and me and Will and Zeke didn't feel like going, so we sat in parking lot, you know?" he says. "And Zeke keeps going on about how he's gonna figure out what Tommy's up to and stop him from going in or some shit like that." Lavias looks around the hall. "Think we can make it outside?"

I shrug. The hall monitors have gotten real strict about letting people in and out of the building. Passing period's almost over, and the halls are starting to clear. We walk down the stairs toward one of the back doors.

"I was thinking, maybe you can talk to him," Lavias says. "'Cause he don't listen to Willy and he don't listen to me. I dunno, maybe I gotta knock some sense into him."

"What makes you think I can talk to him?" I ask.

"Maybe he'll listen to you. I dunno," Lavias says. "But this shit can't keep going on, you know?"

Luckily, it's a tiny little home ec teacher or something stationed at the back door. We walk by her.

"You all can't leave the building," she says.

We just walk out as she yells after us. But what can she do, anyway? It really sucks, when you think about it, how teachers don't get any kind of respect from anybody. I'd sure as hell never want to be a teacher.

The sun is bright outside as we head out to the parking lot. I squint a little, looking toward Ezekiel's Blazer, which is parked sort of in the back of the lot, near the street. We pass a blue Cabriolet that I think is Leandrea's, but I try to shut her out of my mind as we walk through the lot.

Ezekiel and Willy aren't there when we get to his car.

"Aw, shit!" Lavias exclaims and kicks one of the tires.

"Where do you think they went?" I ask, shading my eyes and looking around. I see City Park across the street, all green grass and trees.

At that point, Willy walks toward us, looking as pissed off as I feel. "Don't bother," he says when he gets closer.

"Whassup?" Lavias asks.

Willy shakes his head, frowning. "I can't deal with

this anymore!" He crosses his arms and stands there. I know this has got something to do with Tommy; I don't even have to wonder about that. But I'm not fed up just yet, like Willy. Yeah, I'm frustrated, wondering if I'm going to have to break something up again, but I can't just walk away. I've got to see it. I've got to see what the hell Ezekiel thinks he can do to get Tommy to change.

I hear some shouts from the park, and I start running toward the noise. As I get closer, I recognize Ezekiel's voice screaming "Get out! Get outta here!"

Underneath this tree, a bloody-looking Mexican kid in a blue T-shirt lies on the ground, sort of dazed-looking. Next to him is a kid I've seen hanging out with Tommy, lying there with a big bruise under his eye and a bloody lip. Ezekiel kicks Tommy's partner in the stomach, like he's finishing the kid off. Then he stands over both of them while Tommy stands there holding his head in his hands.

Ezekiel looks from Tommy to his partner, and I see that Ezekiel's holding something shiny in his hand. It looks like a switchblade. "What, were you gonna cut that kid up or something? Who put you up to it? Was it Marcus?" he yells.

Neither Tommy nor his partner answer. Tommy takes deep, controlled breaths, like he's about to blow any minute. His partner lies there on the ground, his skinny arms wrapped around his stomach like he's in pain.

Then Lavias walks up and looks from Ezekiel to Tommy to the guys on the ground. "What the hell—" he says.

Now Ezekiel turns around. He glances at us quickly, looking fierce, but it's almost like he doesn't even see us. "This's between me and Tommy." He turns to glare at Tommy. "I ain't gonna let you do this, man."

"Fuck you!" Tommy screams. "Why the hell do you keep messing with me, huh?"

"I said I ain't gonna let you do this!" Ezekiel says again. "Did Marcus tell you and that punk there to beat up that kid, huh? So you gotta do everything he tells you to now?"

"Fuck you!" Tommy screams again and gives Ezekiel a hard shove.

But Ezekiel doesn't even stagger. "All right, you wanna take somebody on, take me on, you little punk!" He gives Tommy these little shoves in the chest to mess with him. "You're such a badass, you take me on, then!"

Tommy stands there for a second, breathing deeply. Those big eyes of his narrow at Ezekiel, looking deadly. I glance at Lavias, but he looks as exasperated and pissed off as I feel. But we can't do anything, not really. Ezekiel's on his own for this one.

Tommy cuffs Ezekiel across the face, and the next thing I know, he and Tommy are rolling on the ground, throwing punches. The Mexican kid scrambles to his feet and goes running out of the park. Then Tommy's partner pulls himself up, still sort of doubled over, and starts cussing out Ezekiel. I can barely hear him over the noise, but he's saying something like "You're gonna get yours, man!" And then he leaves, too.

But Lavias starts yelling at Ezekiel and goes to stand over them, like he's trying to figure out a way to pull them apart. Finally he grabs Ezekiel by the scruff of his neck and yanks him away from Tommy.

Ezekiel turns on him in a flash. "Butt out," he says in a real low voice. Spit collects in the corner of his mouth. "Don't make me get into it with you, too."

Lavias throws up his hands and takes a step back, like he knows it's not worth it. Ezekiel looks like he could kill somebody. I've never seen him this pissed-off-looking. I watch him turn around to Tommy once more, who pulls himself up to his feet. The two of them stand there for a second, glaring at each other.

"I didn't wanna do that," Ezekiel says finally.

Tommy stands there staring Ezekiel down. He's nothing but blood and breath and eyes. Ezekiel stares back, but there's no way he can match the intensity in Tommy's eyes.

"I'm trying to help you; don't you see that?" Ezekiel

exclaims. And he sounds so much like the reverend it scares me.

"I don't give a shit about you!" yells Tommy.

Ezekiel stands there without moving. Something falls in his face, and he blinks. And in his face I see the reverend's all broken down, like he looks when he can't reach Ezekiel.

Tommy doesn't stop. "What, you think I ain't big enough to do nothing for myself? You think you gotta be my father or something? Well, I ain't about your program." He shakes his head. "I don't give a shit about you."

Ezekiel's mouth softens and his shoulders relax, sinking slowly, like they've deflated or something. "I wanna help you."

I wish he hadn't said that. I hear a soft sigh. Maybe it came from me.

"Fuck your help!" Tommy screams, and Ezekiel loses it again.

"So this is what you're about? Doing what other people tell you to do when you're too stupid to know you could be dead in a year? What kind of shit's that, huh?" Ezekiel sounds more and more like himself, enough to piss me off all over again. "You're nothing but a stupid kid. I shouldn't have wasted my time." He begins to turn away.

"You sonofa—" The word doesn't even get out before Tommy jumps on Ezekiel again. But this time Tommy cracks him one right in the temple, hard enough to make Ezekiel fall down. As they roll there on the ground, I hear the sound of a car engine pulling up to the curb, not too far away. And then I see Marcus and a couple of his homeboys and Tommy's partner, the one Ezekiel beat up. I guess he must've gone to get Marcus.

I close my eyes a second, not wanting to see what's going to come next.

I open my eyes to see Ezekiel untangling himself from Tommy. He stands up slowly, his eyes on Marcus alone. Marcus stands there with three or four other guys. I see one of them holding what looks like a piece of pipe that glints in the sunlight. I swallow, my mouth feeling dry.

Everything gets real quiet. Marcus's homeboys stand there, looking like they're itching to jump on Ezekiel. Tommy's partner stands there trying to look all tough, like he knows he's got five guys backing him up. And Tommy gets up and puts that I'm-the-shit look on his face, too, even though he stands right where he is. I even see him smiling a little, like he knows Ezekiel's going to get his.

Ezekiel points a finger in Marcus's face, but Marcus simply looks him up and down, expressionless. The corners of his mouth turn up a little, for no reason at all, really. All I can think is, Jesus, I don't even know what to think anymore. I can't think anymore.

Ezekiel glares at Marcus, his eyes full of hate. But it's desperate hate. I-don't-understand hate. Little-kid hate. "And you. This is all your fault, man! You're nothing! You're shit!"

Marcus shakes his head and laughs. "You don't get it, do you? I mean, you really don't get it."

I glance at Lavias, who wears a real funny look on his face. Like he doesn't know whether to feel sorry for Ezekiel or to be mad at him.

Almost blind in his anger, Ezekiel runs to shove Marcus. "Can't even stand up for yourself, can you, you mother—"

"ZEKE!" I scream, but I hear the first hollow, echoing sound of a fist and my heart falls from my chest. In an instant, Ezekiel and Marcus are into it, and something changes in Marcus's face. That easy-riding grin of his is gone, replaced by a look that's systematic and fierce, and I know he could kill Ezekiel if he wanted to. But I just watch as some of Marcus's homeboys start shouting at Ezekiel, too, looking like they're about to jump in. Almost like a reflex, Lavias goes running in and starts having it out with one of the guys. I wonder where my reflexes are, why I just stand there like I'm paralyzed or something. Something else gets my attention, and I see about four or five Mexican guys wearing blue shirts come running up. The kid Tommy and his partner beat up points at them, and then guys in blue jump in and I can't tell what's what anymore. I stand there, backed up against the tree, not really knowing what to do.

Marcus bashes Ezekiel's head into the ground while Lavias slugs it out with one of Marcus's homeboys. And then Tommy gets into it with the Mexican kid. It's all one big, shapeless black thing, separating into little islands of black and blue, then blending together. All of a sudden I hear some guy yelling at me in Spanish, and the next thing I know I'm taking him on, throwing punches like a maniac. I can't tell who's who anymore and I don't give a shit. I feel my senses slipping away from me as I keep throwing my fists around, almost blindly. And then I feel something smack my temple. My eyes go out of focus and everything blends together in my head. And then, in the middle of all of it, I hear a couple of loud cracking sounds, sort of like firecrackers.

But then I realize it isn't firecrackers because everything just stops.

Tommy lies on the ground, sort of dazed-looking. Something dark and thick collects at the corner of his mouth, then dribbles in a fat black-red stripe down his chin onto the ground. All the guys, and I guess there are about ten or so, just stand there a second, looking at Tommy, like nobody knows what to do.

A few of the Mexicans start backing away, and I hear

one of them mumble, "Aw, shit." And I wonder why nobody hollers, nobody runs. But time has stopped somehow, this one moment stretching out, terrifyingly slow, like a VCR in frame-by-frame. I glance at Marcus and see him looking down at Tommy on the ground, frowning a little. But he doesn't move either. I look at Lavias, who opens and shuts his mouth over and over again, like he doesn't know what to say.

And then my eyes catch Ezekiel, just ten feet from me.

He's got this funny look on his face, but he isn't looking down at Tommy like everybody else is. He scratches at his neck, first with one hand, then with both. It takes me a second to realize his hands are covered with blood. He twitches a little, his eyes open wide, shock frozen on his face. He sways for a moment, like his legs have turned into columns of sand, and then they collapse underneath him as he falls to the ground, motionless.

"Zeke?" I ask curiously, still not really getting it. I see a dark circle forming on the ground beside him and I gasp, the air searing my lungs.

I just stare at him and he stares at me, like we're the only two people out here. Something flickers in his eyes, something that looks like fear. He opens his mouth a second, looking like he wants to cry out, but no sound comes out.

But the moment ends, like all moments do, and suddenly I'm aware of footsteps, running footsteps, and then the sound of cars zooming away from the curb. Thunder, then silence.

"Aw, shit," Lavias says, his voice shaking. He kneels down to Ezekiel and grabs his face, like he's about to slap him. He hovers over Tommy and Ezekiel, like he doesn't know what to do with himself. He grabs one, then the other. "C'mon, don't do this!" he yells. "Don't do this, don't—"

Once again I hear footsteps, and then I see different faces, white and black and Asian faces. Voices surround me but I can only pick out random words. Words like "oh, my God" and "what happened?" And I hear screams, screams so loud that all I can think is I wish whoever it is would shut up. I look around for Leandrea. I want her to be here. I want her to be here and everybody else to just disappear so we could go someplace where none of this ever happened. But I don't see her. I don't see anything but faces and I don't hear anything but screams. Somebody's grabbed me, trying to ask me questions, but I can't decipher the words. It's all a big mess that spins out of control in my head. I bring my hands to my head to try to stop the spinning.

"Shut up!" I hear myself screaming. "Just shut up! Shut up!" I can barely hear myself over the noise. And then flashing lights invade my peripheral vision and I hear a high, wailing sound as more people come running toward us, people in uniforms who make everybody stand back while they lean down to Tommy and Ezekiel, putting each of them on a stretcher and then wheeling them into an ambulance, away from here.

"Oh, God, Zeke—" Whether I say this aloud or just think it, I don't know anymore. Black spots appear in front of my eyes. I bring my hands in front of my face, like I can push those spots away, but they grow larger and larger, combining themselves with the screaming and the sirens that swirl around me, through me. I can feel the energy draining out of my body, just flowing out into nowhere, and I slip into a black void where all of the sounds and visions die.

Chapter 12

SOMETHING POUNDS AT MY HEAD. MY HANDS SOMEHOW find my eyes, and I grind my knuckles against my brow, willing the pounding in my head to stop. I smell ammonia, which makes my nose wrinkle and my stomach turn. I try to turn over, and my head collides with something hard and cold. I wince and lie down, watching little black spots dance around on a field of white over my head. That's when I figure out that I'm lying on a hard, narrow bed, staring at a ceiling. I sit up, swinging my legs over the side of the bed. I blink a few times to let my eyes adjust to the stark whiteness of the room. I'm in a hospital room. A big metal cabinet sits next to the bed, which I must've hit my head on when I tried to turn over. It takes me a minute to realize that someone's right here with me. Something cold and stinging presses against my cheeks and the corner of my mouth, making me wince again. I rub my eyes and then I'm looking at a youngish-looking white guy wearing a green smock. A shiny stethoscope hangs around his neck, and I stare at it so that I don't have to look him in the face.

"What's your name?" he asks me.

"Todd Williams," I mumble.

"How old are you, Todd?"

"Sixteen."

"What's your address?"

I feel myself frowning. "Why are you asking me this?"

"Just making sure you don't have a concussion."

"Why would I have a concussion?"

The doctor smiles a little. "You fainted."

"Fainted?"

"Your friends carried you in. You've been out for about twenty minutes now," the doctor says.

I turn away from him, embarrassed. I fainted?

"How're you feeling?" he asks.

"Fine," I mumble, but I feel like shit.

"Your friends are in the waiting room," he says, but he's still got a look on his face like he feels sorry for me. That look makes me feel edgy. Nervous. But I don't say anything about it. I let him help me out of bed, and I follow him down the hall to the waiting room.

I stand in the doorway for a minute. Willy and Lavias sit directly across from where I'm standing. Willy stares at the ground, but I can see his face all knotted up, like he's worried. Lavias looks a mess. Both eyes are bruised and his mouth's cut, which makes me wonder how I must look. I run my tongue over my lips, and my mouth feels tender and raw. Then my idiot brain remembers that Ezekiel and Tommy probably are holed up somewhere in this place.

To my diagonal, the reverend sits slumped over in a chair, with Zechariah and Isaiah sitting next to him, their hands holding on to his arms like they're trying to support the guy. Aunt Lorraine sits there holding on to Jeremiah, sobbing. I look away real fast. For a second I think of Aunt Jessie's funeral, seeing the reverend slumped over like that, not even listening to the service, his face frozen downward just like it is right now. I swallow hard. I feel my eyes darting around the room to avoid looking at him, because it'll really do me in to see his face. And I think about Ezekiel laid out somewhere in this place, if he's okay or if he's not, if he's alive or if he's . . . well, he can't be dead or anything, can he? And then I get real sad, deep sad.

"You okay, man?"

I look up quickly. Willy's staring at me. He tries to grin, but it doesn't work and his face sort of fades.

I half shrug, half shake my head and grunt something in reply. I sink into one of the chairs. "Who—wha—" I can't even form complete thoughts.

"I don't know, man," Willy says, like he knows what I'm asking. "I didn't see it. I was sitting out in the parking lot, and then I heard the shots." He stops, like he's run out of words.

"I didn't see, either," Lavias says. "So much going on, you know? I don't know who did it. We already talked to the cops. They was waiting for you to come around." He falls silent and stares into space. That lazy eye of his makes him look half crazy as he sits there without moving, a big old hulk of a guy sitting like all his strength just up and left him.

I look down at my hands again because I don't want to talk to anybody.

Finally, after what seems like forever, another doctor comes out and takes Reverend Washington and Aunt Lorraine into another room. I look up when they leave, but I don't try to follow them or anything like that. I'm worn out. Willy sits at the edge of his seat, even though Lavias doesn't move. Willy gets up and goes to the door.

"I can't hear anything," he says, even though nobody says anything back. Seeing everybody more tensed up starts something in me. I can hardly breathe, like I have a golf ball stuck in my throat. And then this weird craziness flashes over me as I keep seeing Ezekiel on the ground, the way he looked at me, like he wanted me to know something, wanted me to see something inside of him. And me, letting something like stupid jealousy over a girl get in the way of being worried about him. How could I really think I didn't give a shit? How could I let myself act like a stupid kid? I sigh and sink my head in my hands. And then Tommy—I can't even think about Tommy. All I see when I think of Tommy is that thick blood running from his mouth, and my head swims.

The door opens and out walks the reverend, holding his head up. I watch him cross the room and stand in front of me. He's looking right at me, so I can't look away. Looking at me like that, does he know what I think of Ezekiel? How I'm feeling about him? All at once I feel downright ashamed, like I was caught doing something I wasn't supposed to be doing.

But then the reverend smiles, with a gentle look on his face that makes me almost lose it then and there. I can even feel my chin shaking a little, even though I don't look away.

"He's gonna be fine." The reverend's voice is barely a whisper, but it's steady.

"Yeah?" My voice sounds squeaky and girlish.

He nods as his eyes sweep all of us. "It was a clean wound. The bullet went straight through his shoulder. And he's got some bruises and a slight concussion. They still don't know about Tommy." He stops for a second, and I can see the pain in his face.

He takes a deep breath. "They also found out Ezekiel has a really high fever."

"He was sick this weekend," I mumble.

The reverend nods stiffly. "Well, the doctors think he has a viral infection, but they're going to run some more tests to be sure. They're keeping him in Intensive Care, but his doctor doesn't have any reason to doubt that he'll recover. He'll be fine." I can see the relief in his face as he turns his head upward for a second and closes his eyes. And I see it, how much a father can feel for a son, no matter what, no matter how crazy that son is or how crazy he feels, and before I know it I'm on my feet and heading out the door, before I do something stupid like cry.

I stand on the sidewalk for a while, taking a few breaths until that tickling feeling in my chest and throat goes away. I'm sort of surprised at how normal the daylight looks. It almost pisses me off to see the sun shining away overhead without a care in the world, like it doesn't give a shit that I'm miserable. The light is strong, so strong that I shield my eyes and sink down to the steps and sit there because I don't know of anywhere else to go.

"Todd?"

I look up to see Leandrea coming from the direction of the parking lot. She hurries toward me, but she does not run. She sits down next to me.

"I guess you know what's up," I say. My voice sounds creaky.

She nods. "I was in history class when I heard the shots. Everybody went crazy, running out of the building and stuff. The teachers couldn't do anything about it. You were there?"

"I didn't see you," I say—almost snap.

"I was so afraid," she says, sort of whispering. "I heard the shots and the first thing I thought was Ezekiel—and then I went downstairs to the Commons and all these people were talking about it and stuff. I ran across the street, but the police were already there and they blocked the area off." She swallows, her hands shaking a little. "Are they—all right?"

She blinks quickly and her breath goes in and out real fast. She's scared as hell, I can tell. I just look at her a second and see in her eyes how much she cares about Ezekiel. "Zeke's gonna be all right," I mumble. "The bullet went through his shoulder."

She exhales quickly, shutting her eyes and bringing her hand to her chest. I see a couple of tears squeeze out from her eyelids, but she doesn't say anything.

I stare at the sidewalk.

"What about Tommy?"

"They don't know," I say, sounding gruff. "I left before they said anything."

"Todd?" I can barely hear her.

I look over at Leandrea. "Yeah?"

"How'd this happen?"

I just sigh. What can I say? What can I really say? "I don't know," I say finally. "I didn't see who pulled the gun."

"Could it have been your brother?"

I think for a minute, trying my damnedest to remember what happened. What was Marcus doing? He was slugging Ezekiel senseless, I remember that. But could he have done it? Could he have really shot Ezekiel, shot his own cousin? Oh, Jesus—

"Todd?"

I blink a few times and turn to Leandrea. She's staring at me with this scared look on her face. I take a deep breath, feeling a knot in my shoulder that starts to ache. I didn't realize I was that tensed up. But I can't stop thinking about it. I don't really have any idea who pulled the gun, but even the thought that it could've been Marcus just—I don't know. It makes everything in me go cold.

"Todd, are you okay?" she asks.

I nod without saying anything. But it couldn't have been Marcus, could it? After I heard the shots, I saw him standing there, too, just like everybody else. Maybe it was somebody else, one of the guys from the other crew, who pulled the gun just to be doing it. I don't know.

"Hey, Todd." She touches my arm, but I flinch and she pulls her hand away.

"Why ain't you in there with Zeke?" My voice sounds really nasty, but I don't even try to cover it up. I don't think I care anymore.

"There's nothing I can do for him."

That surprises the crap out of me. "What do you mean?"

Leandrea stares toward the mountains. "Because he's hurt now and everything. I don't know what to think about anything. None of this makes any sense, you know?"

What can I say to that? I stare at the asphalt.

"Yesterday, after church, I guess he had a fight with his dad or something," Leandrea says. "His dad told him to stay out of it with Tommy."

"What, he call you or something?"

"No, he came over to my house. He was angry from the second he walked in. So I took him up to my room, asked him what was wrong, and he just started into the whole thing. I guess his dad said something like 'I'll talk to your cousin if you want me to,' and that really set him off. I guess he called his dad a sellout who won't do anything that'll take him off his pedestal. That wasn't what he said, but that's what I got out of it, anyway. I can't remember his exact words. It didn't really make sense. And he was yelling,

yelling at me like I was Reverend Washington or something."

I grin a little at that, in spite of myself. I knew he'd start taking his shit out on her eventually.

"So then I tell him that I'm sorry he's upset. I tell him to lower his voice because he's yelling—" she says.

"What then?"

"Then he shut up about it. And we just sat there for a while, not saying anything. I wanted to ask him why he feels so angry at his dad and stuff. I mean, his dad seems so nice. And I thought, maybe I could understand, because my dad's like that, too, you know?"

That surprises me. "Your dad's like the reverend?"

Leandrea shakes her head quickly. "My dad seems like he's one thing, but he's really something else. If you didn't know my dad, you'd think he was a really nice guy. And so I was wondering if the reverend was like that." She clears her throat. "Different underneath the surface."

"What's your dad like?" I ask her.

"I'm the only child and stuff, so I always got a lot of attention. But at the same time, neither one of my parents ever told me anything important."

"What do you mean?"

"My dad's always bought me a lot of things. He wanted me to have the best of everything," Leandrea says. "But he never really told me what it meant to be black. I think he thinks, 'I go to a black church and I make donations to the Urban League, so I don't have to do anything else.' Every time he watches the news he puts down black people, talks about ghetto niggers and stuff. So I thought that being black was something bad. My dad always talks about how my mom's the prettiest woman in the world. When I was little I used to be kind of jealous of my mom, because I was never going to look like she did, you know? But then Dad would take me into his lap and say things like 'You've got blue eyes, too,' and 'You have long hair, too,' to make me feel better."

She starts talking faster and faster. I just listen.

"My dad, he thinks you have to act white to be successful. But my mom, she isn't enough, you know? I know he's had affairs. I think my mom knows, too, but she doesn't say anything about it. She came from a poor family, so my dad takes care of her and stuff. And it's sick, the way she just—takes it without fighting back. Like, she isn't even a real blonde, but she dyes her hair to keep my dad happy. He loves dressing up and going out with her, showing her off and stuff."

She frowns.

"And then this morning, my dad got into it with me

about Ezekiel, how he didn't think Zeke was good enough for me and stuff. It really made me sick. I just left. I was so mad. I mean, who the hell is he to say who's good enough or not?" Her voice rises and she sounds really pissed off.

"Damn." I don't know what else to say.

Leandrea's quiet for a minute before she speaks again. "I mean, what kind of a jerk am I, if I can't even talk to my own mother? I can't even remember the last time we had a serious conversation. It's like I don't even know how to talk to her anymore, to make her understand me." She cuts herself off, taking a deep breath.

"And I think, is my dad really happy the way he is?" Her voice gets a little shaky, but she doesn't cry or anything. "I mean, sometimes I see him at church and he just looks so sad, like he knows something's missing, but he doesn't do anything about it, you know? And so it made me think, I don't want to be like that. I started reading all these books about Marcus Garvey and Malcolm X and Zora Neale Hurston and stuff. I don't want to be ashamed of being black! And that's what I saw in Ezekiel."

"What?" I ask, not entirely getting what she's saying.

Leandrea stares at the ground. "He isn't afraid of anybody, you know? He's not afraid to start yelling when he feels like it or to say something that he knows'll make people mad. But then again, I don't know. Maybe I just made him into something I wanted him to be."

"So what happened?" I ask again.

"Yesterday?" she says, and sighs. "Well, he was yelling about his dad and everything, saying his dad wasn't a real man and stuff, and I wondered if he wants his dad to show him what it is to be a man, just like I want my dad to show me what it is to be black."

I blink a couple of times at that. The girl is deep.

"And so I tried to talk to him about it," she goes on, crossing her legs under her. "But maybe I didn't do it right, I don't know. I said something like, why can't our fathers be what we need them to be? But he wasn't really listening to me."

"Why not?"

She smiles a little. "I guess because we were sitting on my bed. He just looked at me, sort of looking me up and down like I was wearing a price tag or something."

I shut my eyes, not really wanting to hear any more.

"Up at the condo, it was so great, you know? Even though he was sick and everything, it was nice because I just felt so close to him, even though we didn't really do anything. But yesterday, he was just looking at me, seriously, like I was some prize, just like my dad looks at my mom, and it really pissed me off! I thought I could just forget about it when he put his arms around me and stuff, but I couldn't. It was a complete turnoff, having him near me. Especially when he tried to act all smooth and stuff. It seemed like nothing I felt, nothing that bothered me, really mattered. He was the only one who mattered. I kept trying to talk to him and stuff and he kept trying to get close to me and then he finally said, 'What the hell's your problem?'"

God, it makes me burn to hear that.

"And that blew it for me," Leandrea says. "I told him to leave. Of course, he gets all mad, like I insulted him or something. But I told him I wasn't some possession. He just laughed and tried to kiss me again, like he hadn't heard a word I said. I threw him off again. So he said, 'All right, then, if that's the way you're gonna be,' and he left."

I don't say anything.

Leandrea sighs. "I thought I'd be all upset when he left. But you know, I didn't feel anything. I went to put a CD in my stereo. Something random, I can't remember what. I sat looking out my window at the street. I think I was singing, too. You know how you never really forget the words to songs, even if you haven't heard them in years? But then I just felt him there, in the room, even though I didn't turn around. I felt him standing there, like he was trying to say he was sorry. But I just sat there, looking out the window, singing along. I couldn't turn around. He blew it, you know? I had to hold my ground, even though part of me wanted to just run over to him and let him put his arms around me. But I couldn't do that. And I started feeling strong, sitting there like that. Stronger than I've ever felt in my life. I was getting ready to explain it all to him, to tell him exactly why I was acting the way I was, to try to get him to really listen to me, but when I turned around again—"

She smiles a little and looks right at me. "He was gone." She looks down and sighs. "Maybe I shouldn't have said all that to you. I mean, it doesn't matter now, with him hurt and all."

I just shake my head. What the hell can I think? Nothing connects in my head. Not Ezekiel, not the reverend, not Leandrea. Without a word, I get up and go into the hospital. She doesn't follow me.

Right away, I see a few cops hanging around the reverend. I sure as hell don't want to talk to them now. So I go to sit by myself in a hallway, away from everybody and everything. Mom and Gerald are here now, sitting with the reverend and Aunt Lorraine. I don't remember them showing up. But I don't want to talk to them. I want to go home in the worst way because I'm tired. Not sleepy or anything like that. Just plain old tired.

Don't-care-anymore tired. Care-too-much tired. I just want to forget about all of this.

I feel myself dozing off and later I dream about the fight. But this time I'm in there, throwing punches at Ezekiel, too, and I'm kicking him in the stomach, over and over and over again, hating him more and more and more until my father, of all people, pulls me off him while Marcus just stands there, laughing his ass off.

Chapter 13

I STAY IN BED ALL DAY TUESDAY AND WEDNESDAY. I
guess I don't want to deal with anything or anybody, especially not Ezekiel. Every time I think of him, I think of
Tommy lying there in the hospital still in limbo, and
what Leandrea told me, and all I can do is hate him,
then hate myself for hating him because he's supposed
to be my best friend and everything.

Reverend Washington comes to see me Wednesday
night. He's over at our house for a prayer meeting with
my mom and Aunt Lorraine and people from the
church. I don't go downstairs to join in or anything like
that. Later on I hear a knock on my door. "Can I come
in?" comes the reverend's voice.

"Yeah," I mutter, even though I really don't want
him to.

He comes into my room and sits down on my bed.
He looks really old to me. The lines in his face that always made him look distinguished now make him look

plain tired. But I guess he's been through a lot. "How've you been, son?"

I shrug. "Okay, I guess."

"I was wondering why you haven't been over to see Ezekiel at the hospital."

I knew he was going to ask that, which makes me feel guilty. So I try to cover it up. "Well, since he's getting better, you know—" But I sound stupid, so I just stare at my old blanket.

"Did something happen between you two?"

I think my silence tells him what he wants to know. I mean, what can I say? Oh, yeah, well, your son's a sonofabitch and I'm sick of his shit?

"Ezekiel asks about you," the reverend says quietly.

I sigh. I know I have to face him sooner or later.

The reverend sighs, too, looking sad. "You know, I just—" He clasps his strong hands together, frowning some. He looks really disturbed. "I've been thinking and thinking, trying for the life of me to figure out all that anger Ezekiel has, where it all comes from."

He looks at me quickly, but I don't say anything.

"I've tried and tried to understand what it's like to be young and angry." He laughs a little. "Believe it or not, I was young and angry once, too, but I guess I channeled that anger into something else."

I remember something Ezekiel said a long time ago. I guess some state senator was over at the reverend's house, making a big fuss over the picture of the reverend with Dr. Martin Luther King. Ezekiel said, "The reverend, he marched with King, but me, I woulda been a Panther."

"And I've felt so torn," the reverend goes on. "I mean, what can I do? How can I tell him it's not right to stand up for something he believes in? How can I say it's wrong to try to help someone, especially someone in the family? I can't do that. That'd be going against every value I've raised him on. It's just his way of going about it that bothers me so much. You know, his—his audacity, I guess you can say, makes me proud in so many ways."

The reverend stops, like he's thinking about something. "And then I just worry," he says after a moment or so. "I worry because I'm afraid this world doesn't have any place for that kind of bravado anymore. Not when so many young people don't understand the value of human life."

I sit there sort of amazed that he's talking with me this way. I see it again, how much Ezekiel means to the reverend, even with all the crazy shit Ezekiel does. The reverend would do anything for Ezekiel. Absolutely anything. I take a deep breath, feeling this strange heaviness in my chest.

The reverend laughs. "Sometimes I think Ezekiel was born in the wrong decade. Or even in the wrong century. And I think part of what bothers him is that he wants something concrete to fight against. In my day, we had the system as our enemy. But now there're so many enemies on the inside, what can we do?" He hangs his head. "What can we do?"

I can't find any words to say.

"I wonder if I've failed him somehow," the reverend says, his head still low. "If I didn't try to understand him from his perspective, instead of from my own, as a parent."

I wonder if I've ever felt as miserable as I feel right now. More than anything, I just feel hopeless. It's the sort of feeling you get when you're watching a TV program about starving kids in Africa, that there's nothing you can do to make things better. But you can flip the channel and then you start thinking about something else. I don't know how to turn away from this. All I know is that I want the reverend to leave. I can't stand it, having him sitting here, caring so much about Ezekiel.

I can't stand him reminding me over and over again that no one's ever going to care that way about me.

"I'll go see Zeke tomorrow," I say, even though I really don't want to.

The reverend stands up and smiles at me. "I know he'll want to see you."

"Do you know how Tommy's doing?"

The reverend looks sad once again. "They still have him on life support. It's all they can do to keep him stabilized. Keep praying for him," the reverend says. "Keep praying for him." And he leaves.

The next morning I get up and take a shower. Nobody's in the house when I come downstairs. I guess everybody's at the hospital.

I sit down at the table and begin to eat Cheerios out of the box. The table is strewn with newspapers, which I guess nobody remembered to throw out. I pick up a paper. The shooting made the front page of the Tuesday paper. I glance over the article. The headline says something about two guys from the other crew being hauled in as suspects. Today's paper has some commentary on the tragedy of gang violence. The cereal in my mouth starts to taste like sawdust, so I put the box down.

I take the bus over to the hospital and sit in a corner until visiting hours start. I don't want to be around anybody. Not Gerald or my mom or Aunt Lorraine and especially not the reverend.

Some girl in a jumpsuit leads me up to Ezekiel's room at around noon or so. I stand outside for a minute, getting my resolve up. When I open the door, Ezekiel's sitting up in bed, looking at a comic book.

"Hey, Todd! Long time no see!" he exclaims. His face is really pale, but his voice is as loud as usual.

I walk in and pull up a chair beside his bed. The room's pretty small but bright because the window faces the sun. All these bouquets of flowers line the windowsill.

"Yeah, I hate all them flowers, too," Ezekiel says, watching me looking at them. "All the ladies from the church sent them over."

"Yeah, they look kinda stupid. How're you feeling?"

"Okay. I wanna get outta here, but they won't let me until this infection clears up, or whatever," Ezekiel says, leaning back on the bed. His arm is in a sling. There's a bandage at his neck and another at his temple, and there are some bluish patches on his cheek and forehead and some black, jagged scars at the corners of his mouth.

"Do you know about Tommy?"

His face falls a little and he nods. "Maybe this'll be it, you know? Maybe this'll show him that gang-banging's stupid—"

"You still onto that?" I say real sharply, before I mean to.

He looks at me sort of suspiciously. "What's your problem?"

I stare at my hands, grabbing one fist and then the other. I don't think it's occurred to him that Tommy might not get up and walk out of here tomorrow or something. It makes me mad, how out of it Ezekiel can be.

"You all right?" he asks.

I shrug without looking up. That loud, demanding voice of his is really starting to piss me off.

"You seen Leandrea anywhere? I thought she'd be here."

I look Ezekiel in the face. "Why the hell should she come see you?"

Ezekiel looks really surprised. "What?"

"I'm serious, man, why the hell should she come see you?"

Ezekiel frowns. "So what are you trying to say, huh?"

I turn away from him and stare at the sink in the corner. For a second I just sit there, feeling his eyes on my back. When I turn around and look at him again, he's staring at me, just as I thought. And all that confusion I felt last night, wondering what I'm thinking of him, all of that clears up. Because I hate him. Right now I really hate the guy. "That you ain't shit."

Ezekiel laughs. "What?"

"You ain't shit," I say again.

Ezekiel stops laughing and his eyes go narrow. "What the—"

"All your talk about your dad being this bootlicker who doesn't do nothing but preach—"

"Why don't you just shut up right now!" Ezekiel snarls.

But that just makes me raise my voice, too. "Maybe

if you opened your eyes and looked at him, you'd see an old guy who really gives a shit about you. And then Leandrea—"

A smug grin comes to Ezekiel's face. "So that's what this is about."

My face heats up a little, but I keep looking him in the face. "She told me all about what happened with you and her."

"So you believe her?" Ezekiel snaps.

"Yeah, I believe her."

Ezekiel raises his eyebrows a little, still wearing that stupid self-satisfied grin. "You just say that 'cause you want her and you're mad that I got her."

I have to take deep breaths so I don't go and knock him out of that hospital bed. I get up and walk over to the window. Ezekiel's room overlooks the front parking lot, so I start staring at the cars driving in and out. "I don't know. But I know she talks to me. I know she feels like she can talk to me and she can't talk to you since you don't listen to nobody. And I know she likes me. I treat her like a person instead of property or something. And I know she hasn't been to see you because she thinks you're a sonofabitch."

"So what, you and her got something going, is that what you came to tell me?" Ezekiel yells back.

His voice makes me turn around to look at him, but I don't say anything.

He lies back against the pillows and throws his comic book down so hard I hear it smack on the floor. "I shoulda known."

"Nah, we don't got nothing going," I say.

Ezekiel cracks his knuckles, staring at his hands like he's thinking about something. He doesn't say anything for a minute. Then he mutters, "Stupid bitch. That's what they all are, you know?" Ezekiel looks up at me like nothing's wrong and we're hanging out at his house.

All I can do is shake my head. "Nah, you don't know."

Ezekiel grins, looking sort of nervous. "But hey, man, we can't let some bitch get between you and me. No girl's worth that—"

I throw up my hands. "You don't get it, do you! This ain't about Leandrea. This is about you!"

"That's what you keep saying, but what're you trying to say?" retorts Ezekiel.

"That you ain't shit because you think you know everything there is to know about people without listening to what they got to say!" I'm practically hissing now. I can't yell anymore. I take a step toward the bed so that I'm standing right over him.

"You think you know it all." I look Ezekiel right in the eyes. "Who's the man and all. Your father, naw, he ain't no man 'cause he's too busy trying to make a name for himself, right? Even though he sat there in the waiting room crying when he thought you might die? Even though he came to me last night talking about how much he wants to get where you're coming from and shit. And my dad hasn't done a damn thing for me in my life, but that's all right since he ain't a real man either, right? But you, you're so damn self-righteous, you can say who's the man and who ain't, right?"

Ezekiel looks so mad that he actually jumps up toward me, but then he lies down and squeezes his eyes shut, like he's in pain.

"You know, I'm just gonna let myself look at you," I say. "For a while I wouldn't. I was afraid I'd hate you. But I don't give a shit anymore."

Ezekiel opens his eyes and stares at me. His eyes are wide with surprise, like he's never seen me before. I don't know; maybe he hasn't.

"And Tommy, you never gave a shit about him. It was never about keeping him out of the posse. It was about keeping him away from Marcus and saying you did it. So everybody can say, 'Look, there's Zeke Washington.'" I sigh. "You think he's just trying to be a badass? You think he's just a punk kid? If you ever talked to him, maybe you'd have known why he really wanted to be down with Marcus. Ever think of that? Naw, man, 'cause you knew it all."

Ezekiel turns on his side, away from me. "What the hell do you know?"

I walk around to the other side of the bed so I'm looking him in the face again. "But did you ever think of just stopping to ask Tommy what's up? Ever think of that?"

Ezekiel doesn't look at me.

I sit down in the chair again, leaning forward so that I'm kind of up in his face. "If you did anything, you pushed him in!"

Ezekiel looks up at me now. When he sits up, I see a growing red stain under the bandage on his neck. Maybe his stitches ripped or something when he tried to jump at me. He doesn't say anything, but that surprised look is still on his face. It's that same wounded expression that I haven't seen since the day his mom died. I suck in my breath and look down at my hands. I almost want to change the subject, to say something stupid to make him laugh so we could just hang out like old times. But I shut that feeling off. I have to. And as I keep talking, that feeling disappears.

"You talked to Tommy like you didn't think he could do nothing for himself," I say, still looking at my hands. "What was the kid supposed to do, huh? What would you do?"

I look up. Ezekiel turns on his side again, like he doesn't want to look at me anymore.

"I know what you'd do," I say. "You'd be running over to Marcus so fast you wouldn't know what hit you. 'Cause you'd have to prove yourself. You'd have to prove you were good enough to be a man, no matter what, right?"

"Get out," he mutters.

"Naw, I ain't done yet." I get up and walk over to the window. Ezekiel scowls at the bedsheets, his face tense.

"You think you know so much and you don't know shit. You really don't, man!" I exclaim. "And you know what's funny? I used to think you were something. You were always doing something, you know?"

Ezekiel sits up quickly and points toward the door. "Get out!"

"But you, you keep trying to look into everybody, acting like you can see all inside people when you can't even see what's on the outside. Not with anybody. And now Tommy's laid up somewhere in here—"

Ezekiel's chest heaves up and down, and I can see the veins popping up from under his temples. "Get the hell outta here!"

I stand there for a minute and we look at each other, both of us breathing heavy. I know he'd love to tear me apart if he could, and I sure as hell would do the same thing. But I back away from him. "I'm gone, man."

I turn and walk out of the room, down to the lobby. And then it really hits me, what I said to Ezekiel. It's like

I talked all my insides out and there's nothing left but this big, gaping hole in my chest. I'm even more tired as I sit by myself in the lobby. I don't want to think; I don't want to feel anything. I just stare at the blank television screen above my head, thankful that I'm alone.

As I'm sitting there by myself, Gerald comes into the lobby and walks right up to me. He shifts his weight around and swallows a couple of times, then looks at me with funny eyes. "Todd, aw, man—" he says.

I turn to face him. "Whassup?"

"It's Tommy, man. He died."

Chapter 14

TOMMY'S DEAD. I SAY THAT TO MYSELF OVER AND OVER again, but I can't seem to connect the image with the word. My head drops and I stare at the table. I reach over to pick up the remote and turn on the television.

Gerald snatches the remote away from me and shuts off the TV with such force I think he might break the damn thing. He turns to glare at me, hands on hips in that how-dare-you look of a parent. "Whassup with you, man, don't you give a shit?" he practically yells.

I blink a few times before I realize how stupid it must've looked to turn on the TV. I rub my temples with my fingers, trying to rub out the pounding in my head.

Gerald jerks me to my feet, giving me a yank on the arm that doesn't feel good at all. His hands grip the sides of my arms so tight I want to wince, but I don't. I'm standing close enough to see into his nostrils, which flare with his anger. "Tommy's dead! He's dead! He's fourteen years old and he's dead!"

"Yeah, yeah," I say, feeling a little faint. "You told me. It's just that—"

"It's just what?"

"Zeke—"

"What's he got to do with anything?"

"Nothing." A deep sadness takes over me as I feel any strength I had leave my body. The sadness comes on so sharp, so sudden, that it hurts. It's not Tommy being dead. That's part of it. It's something else. Something deeper and harder to get to than that.

Gerald lets go of me, and I sink onto the couch, wanting to roll up in a ball and disappear so I don't have to feel anything anymore. I want Leandrea to be here and hold me in her lap like she held Ezekiel. I want Ezekiel, Lavias, Willy, and me to be sitting around on the basketball court, goofing off and doing nothing. I don't know what I want.

Gerald sits down next to me. I look out the window at the parking lot, but Gerald starts talking anyway. "A blood clot went to his brain or something."

All of a sudden I hear a loud, sharp cry coming from the other room that scrapes at my insides. It's a woman's cry. A mother's cry. I want to get up and get out of here like God knows what.

"Oh, Jesus," Gerald mutters. "Jesus."

I keep staring out the window as the cry turns into a steady sobbing, with other female voices joining in.

There's something in the pit of my stomach. A strange sensation. Hot. Like someone's poking at me with one of those things you stick in the fireplace. I forget what they're called, but it burns.

"Hey, Todd. You okay?"

I just shrug. "It's too bad." That's not what I mean, though. Not at all. I can't even find words to say what I mean, words that describe this burning inside of me, so bad I can't stand it. I can almost feel the flames themselves, licking at my stomach, my intestines, all the goop that's wound up in there.

But Gerald can't see what's going on inside my head or my stomach, so he just looks at me funny. "Yeah," he says, sounding sarcastic. "It is too bad."

I suddenly think of Marcus, trying to remember how he reacted when he heard the gunshot. He'd just stood there, hadn't he? I can't remember anything about the way he looked, no matter how hard I try. "Is Marcus here?" I ask.

Gerald's eyes go narrow. "I can't believe you just asked that. Damn! All the time that kid spent around Marcus. Didn't he know what that would do?"

I don't say anything else, but I can't help but wince at his words. The words are hollow. Empty. Because this time it wasn't Marcus. But I can't think of any way to tell Gerald that this time he can't just blame Marcus. The whole thing's a lot more complicated than that. All of a sudden I want to see Ezekiel again. No, I need to see Ezekiel again. I wonder if he knows Tommy's dead. Maybe he does, but I want him to hear it from me.

I almost run into a nurse on my way up the stairs to Ezekiel's room. I throw open the door without knocking.

Ezekiel's sitting up in bed, the back of his head motionless as he stares out the window.

He turns around quickly as I come in, but he doesn't say anything to me. He's got a strange look frozen on his face, halfway between terror and disbelief. I know that he knows.

"Yo, Zeke," I say. My voice cracks a little and I clear my throat.

He doesn't move.

"Tommy's dead, man." My voice sounds so strange when I say that. It sounds gravelly, like I'm ninety years old or something.

Ezekiel's head lowers some and his shoulders twitch. "I know."

I put my hands in my pockets. "Who told you?"

"My dad." His voice sounds flat, too. "Just a minute ago."

"Oh." I keep shifting my weight, not knowing what to say or do. It takes everything in me to pick up my feet and put them down again enough times so that I'm practically standing over Ezekiel.

"Wanna say I did it?" Ezekiel says, his eyes narrowing

at me. "Wanna say, 'Zeke, man, you might as well've pulled the trigger yourself! It's your fault!'"

The muscles in my face and neck get real tight, like somebody put me in a pressure cooker or something.

"Then why don't you say it?" Ezekiel's shouting now. "You said I ain't shit; say it again, goddamnit! Tell me I didn't give a shit about Tommy and I was only in it for myself or whatever the hell it was you said before!" He reaches up to grab me by the neck of my shirt and jerk me down to eye level with him. My feet slip from underneath me and I jam my knee against the bed, which makes me gnash my teeth together. I try to pull away from him, but his grip tightens. I feel myself breathing in short little breaths. I can't do anything but look right into his eyes.

"Why don't you kick my ass, then," Ezekiel hisses at me, his breath hot on my face. "I know you want to. Why don't you just do it. Do it!" He screams right into my ear, making me wince. I wrench myself away from him and sit down in the chair by the bed. Ezekiel clenches his hands into fists and shuts his eyes so tight that the veins pop out from his neck. A low sound rises from his throat, like a kettle right before it whistles.

All I can do is look at him.

Ezekiel hunches over and grabs the top of his head, taking handfuls of dreadlocks into his fists, and for a second it looks like he's going to rip his hair from his head. His hands shake and then I realize his whole body's shaking, like something inside of him's about to bust wide open.

But then he slumps back against the bed and his hands fall to his sides. He looks exhausted. The color drains from his face until he just looks pale and small. His eyes drop to the sheets and his head hangs, like it weighs a hundred pounds or something. His shoulders heave some, and it takes me a minute to realize he's crying. He doesn't even attempt to wipe the tears from his face, letting them spill down his cheeks onto the blanket. I stand up slowly and take a step toward him, but I don't know why. That hole in my chest only grows deeper and deeper until I just feel numb and dead all over. I stand there watching him feel what I know I have to be feeling, too, somewhere down there inside where I can't get to, somewhere underneath all this numbness. I let my eyes fall to the dingy linoleum floor, shame growing over the numbness, and with the shame, disgust. I shouldn't have come back to see Ezekiel.

Ezekiel stops crying and just sits there, dazed-looking, scared-looking. He looks the way I've felt so many times when I'm alone up in my room, thinking about all the things that bug me about who I am. More than anything, he looks alone.

"Why don't you get outta here. I don't got nothing to say to you," Ezekiel says flatly.

I turn around and leave without looking back.

I trudge down to the lobby, unable to lift my eyes from the ground. My head feels heavy and swollen, like my neck's too weak to support it. And then my chest feels all caved-out and empty. I'm tired, more tired than I've ever been in my life. All I want to do is go home and go to bed, to shut all of this out and hope once more, like I've been hoping the last few mornings when I open my eyes, that all of this will be nothing more than a dream after all and everything can go back to the way it used to be.

I walk out of the hospital and just keep walking, my eyes down. I only look up one time, and that's because I hear the loud blare of a horn honking and the screeching sound of tires. I guess I'd walked out into the middle of a road without looking. But I'm too worn out to even care. Some guy leans out his car window and starts cussing at me, but I just keep walking.

I don't even realize where I am until I've walked myself all the way home. I fish my keys out of my pocket to open the front door, but then I realize it's already open.

Marcus sits in the living room by himself, watching TV. I just look at him, seeing him sprawled out on the couch. He looks like he always does: saggy jeans that don't cover up how skinny he is, Raiders cap cocked ass-backward, and some stupid T-shirt. I glance at the

TV and see some fat guy stirring something on a stove, and for a second I wonder like an idiot when Marcus got into cooking shows. But then I look at him again and see his eyes sort of glazed over, like he's not paying attention to the TV.

"Tommy's dead." My voice sounds flat and cold.

Marcus doesn't do anything to acknowledge that he heard me.

"Ain't you gonna say something?" I ask.

He shrugs. "What'm I supposed to say?"

"Ain't you sorry about it?"

"Yeah."

"But don't you—" I stop because he's not looking at me. "You really don't give a shit, do you. I mean, you don't give a shit about nothing."

Marcus turns around to look at me, and I'm kind of surprised because it seems like for the first time, he's really looking at me, even though his face stays blank. But he looks right into my eyes, like he can see everything inside and he knows better. "What do you want me to say? Should I play taps for the kid? Should I be boo-hooing like I'm his ma or something? I'm sorry, but it ain't my fault."

"How can you say it's not your fault!" I practically shout.

Marcus shakes his head slowly. "You want me to say it's too bad? All right, I'll say it. It's too bad."

I stare at him, looking for some sign of—something. But he remains still. "So that's it," I say. "You just don't give a shit about nothing or nobody."

Marcus takes a deep breath, but he still doesn't look bothered. "I don't got any say in what you think, man."

I'm getting frustrated. "Then how can you sit there like it's nothing, huh? That kid came to you—"

"Yeah, he came to me and I gave him what he wanted."

"You think that's what he really wanted?" I'm screaming now. "To be dead? You know, you're really full of shit!"

Marcus looks sort of taken aback, like he never expected me to say anything like that. But then I see the corners of his mouth twitch, like he thinks I'm not serious. And that makes something start burning in me, burning right in that big hole in my chest. I think of Ezekiel laid up in the hospital, the way he looked when he let go of me and just lay there in his bed, like he couldn't do any more. And I look at Marcus sitting there like nothing bothers him, like he doesn't have to be responsible for anything or anybody, and something blows inside of me.

"Get out," I say.

Now he looks at me like I'm the one who's lost it. "What was that?"

"I said get out!" I say again, louder this time. "I'm sick

of your shit, the way you come around here acting like you don't give a shit about anybody. Why the hell do you come around, then?"

Marcus just looks at me, expressionless.

"What, you wanna throw it in our faces, huh?" I go on, my chest heaving. "You wanna piss off Mom and Gerald and everybody else 'cause we ain't like you?"

Marcus stands up slowly, but he starts to look amused in a way that only makes me madder, makes me want to knock that look right off his face.

"I'm sick of your shit!" I get all up in his face, challenging him. "You don't give a shit about nobody 'cause you're too damn afraid to. Why don't you just get the hell out and don't come back!"

Marcus throws up his hands, looking like he doesn't want to be bothered. Like he has something better to do. He turns around and walks away. I stand there a minute looking after him as he goes out to sit on the back porch. And then this rage rushes up to my head, knocking down all my reason and sending me flying after Marcus. "I ain't finished with you!" I scream. As I tear through the house, that rage pushes my legs, puts strength into my arms, more than any I've ever had before. Right now I feel like I could kill somebody with my bare hands.

Marcus is sitting on the back porch, holding a pipe in his hands that he looks like he's about to light, but he turns around as I pull open the screen door, so hard the damn thing comes off its hinges.

I stand there for a minute, hating him more than I ever thought I hated Ezekiel, or my father. I hate the way he sits there like nothing's up. I hate the way he always sits there like that. I want him to be as pissed off as I am. I want him to feel what I felt when I stood there in Ezekiel's hospital room. I guess that's why I pull him to his feet, knocking the pipe out of his hands.

Marcus laughs for a second before I cuff him across the jaw. Then his eyes cloud over and he throws me one back, hard enough for me to hear his fist on my face, but that just makes me even madder.

"You don't give a shit about nothing!" I scream, throwing him everything I got. I'm missing a lot, I know, because I'm wasting more energy on the air than on him.

After a while I don't know what I'm screaming anymore, but I'm fighting him, fighting everything that pisses me off, confuses me about him, trying to get him mad, trying to get him to hate me as much as I hate him, trying to get him to feel what I know he feels, has to feel. He fights back; I feel it in quick, sharp pain in my jaw, my stomach, and once he gets me to the ground, in the pounding of my head against the cement. But our patio's cement's so soft from age it doesn't feel much harder than grass. I feel a dull ache in my head that bursts with knifing little pains at each hit. I see Marcus's face above me as he pounds my head on the ground, his face going in and out of focus. He looks intent on what he's doing, his face set in a frown, but he's not hating me. He's just fighting back, then kicking my ass on top of it to show me what a fool I was to take him on. And somewhere in my messed-up head I remember something he said to me once. Never fight when you're really mad, because that's when you'll lose. And I feel the strength leave my arms and legs as I lie there on the ground like spaghetti.

Marcus sits up. I guess he realizes it's over. All I hear is the raspy sound of his chest rising and falling as he slowly stands up. He looks down at me with something like pity, but then his face clouds over and he jerks me by the arm to my feet. My head hurts so much I stand there swaying a minute, unsure if my wobbly knees'll hold me up. I stand there looking him in the eye, feeling all my anger melt down to nothing. I feel like nothing. Marcus just looks at me, like he wonders what's up, even though he doesn't ask.

Finally he shakes his head and grins a little. "Man, you come up behind people like that, you're liable to get yourself killed," he says, then bends down to pick up the cap that fell off his head. "And nobody wants to see that." He turns and walks away, back into the house, I guess. But I don't follow him. I stand there where I am, another rush coming over me like the rush of anger I had before. But this feeling pulls at me, pulls at my roots until I don't know what's up and what's down and none of it means anything anyway. And I start to cry, right there where I'm at. I stand there and cry like I'm two years old, and when I can't stand anymore, I fall to the ground and cry, really bawl, like I haven't done since I don't remember when. I just bury my face in the dirty cement, feeling the breeze skip over me, and I sob like there's no tomorrow, and then I think that maybe there isn't one and then I can't think anything anymore as my tears drown out my thoughts, putting out the flames.

Chapter 15

TOMMY'S FUNERAL IS ON THE FOLLOWING WEDNESDAY after. Reverend Calhoun, an associate minister, delivers the service, and I sit between my mom and Gerald. Reverend Washington sits in front of us with Aunt Lorraine, his arm tense around her shaking shoulders. He doesn't move except to lower his head every now and then, like it's too heavy for his neck to hold it up.

My mom cries. A few tears fall down her face and she brushes them away, real gently. Just watching Mom sit there, trying to hold in all her pain while some of it escapes down her face, makes me feel really sorry for her. I can't help but think how hard it must be to be the mother of sons. Because once they hit twelve, you can't talk to them anymore. Not really. I've never thought about it like that before. I want to do something for her, but the only thing I can think of to do is to take her hand. Her hand is small, sort of soft, but I feel the calluses on her fingers from typing all the time. She doesn't say anything to me, or even look my way, but she squeezes my hand to let me know she appreciates it. Gerald sits there stiffly, his thick neck tight like he's trying to keep something in. Toni and Kinesha sob quietly next to him. Behind us a bunch of girls sob loudly enough to make me uncomfortable. Girls from the neighborhood Tommy hung out with and stuff. I sit there wishing they'd shut up so that we could all just sit there and be quiet, but then I get mad at myself for thinking that. I'm at a funeral, I tell myself. A goddamned funeral. I make myself look at the coffin, all dark and shiny, looking like a piece of nice furniture. If it weren't for all the white flowers spilling over the top, I could probably forget what it really is, even with all of the people here and all of the crying. If it weren't for those damned flowers, I wouldn't have to think that Tommy was lying in there dead, wearing a black suit, his hair combed all nice, his skin hard and waxy-looking, sort of like the fake fruit my mom keeps in a bowl on the dining room table. I spent maybe three minutes at the viewing yesterday. I went up to the front of the chapel, looked at him lying there so still and unnatural-looking, and then I went home. I don't know; it seems so morbid to me, the whole idea of a viewing. I don't really see why people spend so much money trying to make dead people look like they're asleep or something. Because no matter how much you dress someone up or comb his hair, the person still looks dead.

I start shifting around because the pew's starting to feel real hard under me. While I'm shifting I see Ezekiel out of the corner of my eye. He's sitting in the pew to the right and sort of diagonally to me. His brothers sit around him, but he's got his good arm crossed over his sling, like in his head he's really all alone. I didn't see him at the viewing yesterday, but I guess he got there after I left. I haven't seen him since last week at the hospital. I heard someone say he got out of the hospital on Sunday. He sits there in a black suit like the one I'm wearing, not really looking at anything, staring into space. I turn to face forward real quick so that I don't have to look at him anymore. I don't even want to think about him. Because I keep seeing how he looked in the hospital when I told him Tommy was dead. I can't get it out of my head, as much as I try. My mouth feels dry, so I swallow, and then I reach up to loosen the collar of my shirt because my throat feels like it's closing up on me.

I watch the reverend stand up, letting go of Aunt Lorraine real gently, settling her on the pew like she's a little kid or something, and then walk up to the pulpit. The church gets real quiet. Too quiet. I wish somebody'd sneeze or something, break all this tension here. I hate funerals. I really, really hate them.

The reverend looks out at all of us for a second and we all look back at him. I want to get up and leave in the worst way. I don't want to hear anybody talk about Tommy. I don't want anybody to say what a great person he was, how smart he was, how much potential he had, all the crap people say when somebody dies, crap nobody'd be saying about him if he were here. I don't want to hear any of it.

But the reverend doesn't look like he's going to say anything like that. In fact, he shifts a little on his feet, looking uncomfortable, like he doesn't know what the hell he's going to say. He clears his throat and opens his mouth like he's going to talk, then shuts it and clears his throat again. I wonder what he's thinking, if maybe he feels responsible somehow for everything that's happened. Maybe that's the edgy feeling I've got crawling around underneath the surface. Or maybe I'm just realizing how much I really didn't know the kid, somebody who was supposed to be family. Or maybe I'm just realizing that Tommy's not going to be coming around the house to hang out with Toni, that I'm not going to see him out on the basketball court acting like a badass, that Ezekiel and Marcus will never fight over him again. Maybe I'm just realizing that Tommy's dead.

The reverend clears his throat one more time. "I don't have any words to say."

The church is silent. The reverend's voice stays really low, without taking on the volume and the power of his sermons, those sermons that lift him from the pulpit and make him seem larger than life. More than anything, Reverend Washington looks like a man. Not a god, not a hero, or anything like that. Just an ordinary man. "I don't have any words that can take away the pain," he goes on. "I don't have any words that can make any sense out of all of this. I don't have any words that can bring this boy back to the world that we know. I don't have any miracles."

His eyes fall to the ground, and he stands there for a second before he speaks again. "No miracles," he says again, his voice even softer now. "It's times like these when we begin to question those things we took for granted before, all those words we say together every Sunday, all those words I say to you. In the face of life's darkest moments, we have to wonder just how strong is that faith, that faith in God that gives us hope, that faith that allows us to face each day that we are given. We know in our minds that tomorrow isn't promised to us. And yet—" He stops again, like he doesn't know what he's going to say next or he doesn't want to say what he had thought he would.

He takes a deep breath. "I can't tell you to gather up all that faith to see yourselves through. I can't tell you that we should be happy that this child now stands before God. I can't tell you to be strong."

His voice breaks a little, and I can see something wet on his face. "All I can say—" He stops a minute, like he's trying to pull himself together. He doesn't even try to look out at the congregation. His head hangs, and I see his shoulders heave up and down. Then he continues. "That child is my nephew. I miss him. I will always miss him, and somehow, some way—"

He clears his throat again. "I have to make my peace with God."

And then he walks away from the pulpit and goes to sit on the front pew by himself, holding his head in those giant hands of his. His shoulders shake, and I realize he is crying. Just sitting there crying by himself, not trying to hide it, play it off, anything. I feel all torn up, watching him. The soft murmur of crying comes in all around me, and I sit there drained, not knowing what to do, what to think, what to feel. From the corner of my eye I see Gerald's head drop and his face crumple, and I turn away. I glance to my right, toward Ezekiel, but I see an empty space between two of his brothers. He's gone.

I don't look up during the rest of the service. I can't. All I can do is sit there reminding myself to breathe as my head feels heavier and heavier.

But then I'm up on my feet and we're all heading out in the recessional. I'm almost blinded by the bright sun as I step out of the church. I stand there for a second while my eyes adjust to the light. It sucks that it's such a beautiful day. April really is a shitty month. Nothing ever happens when it's supposed to. It snows for people's outdoor weddings and it's sunny when people die. What makes it all worse is the zoo of people out in front. Television cameras, reporters sort of standing back, looking at everybody. Every now and then, some pointy-nosed woman pulls aside a kid to put on camera and talk about Tommy. It's so predictable. And on the five o'clock news, they'll say that Tommy was the next victim of gang-related violence. And they'll have some black preacher on there saying that the kid needed a father figure. Then they'll have some white cop get on and say the kid needed a better environment. Then the pasty-faced anchorwoman will shake her head and call it a tragedy, and the anchorman with too much makeup will agree. End of story.

I glance around for Ezekiel, but he's probably long gone. Then I ask myself what difference that makes. He's the last person I'd want to see anyway. I get sort of nauseous as Gerald and the other pallbearers lift the coffin into the hearse. I scratch my throat, feeling suffocated all over again. And then I realize I'm going to throw up if I don't get out of here. So I sneak around to the side of the church, avoiding everybody, and start walking home.

When I get home, I see a big, beat-up-looking white convertible g-ride sitting in front of the house. The car sits so low to the ground you'd probably fall on your butt trying to get out of the driver's seat if you weren't careful. A lot of guys around here have cars like that, but I've never seen this one before. Then it hits me and I shake my head at my own stupidity. It's Marcus. Who else can it be? I sigh and trudge up the front lawn to the door. I stand there on the porch a second, wondering if I should even go in.

Then the door opens and I'm standing face-to-face with Marcus.

He raises his eyebrows a little, like he wasn't expecting to see me. He's holding a pile of stuff in his arms. Clothes, it looks like. He brushes by me and I watch him walk down the yard and dump the pile into the backseat. I smell something as I go by him, something smoky. I blink a few times, my head spinning a little, and I realize it's weed. I can't stand the smell of weed.

Marcus walks back up to the house and goes inside. When he steps into the doorway, he turns to me. "You gonna stand there staring at me all day?"

I go into the house and fall onto the living room couch. I lie there, hearing Marcus's footsteps as he goes downstairs to the basement. When he lived here, he used to have a room down there. Mom had the basement refinished a long time ago so Gerald and Marcus wouldn't have to share a room. Now I think Mom uses Marcus's old room as a place to store all her junk. I didn't know Marcus still had any stuff down there, but he comes back upstairs and crosses the living room with another armful of stuff.

"What're you doing?" I ask him as he's about to walk out the door.

He stops and turns around to look at me. "Getting some stuff," he says, and then he grins a little. "Got a problem with that?"

I don't say anything, and he walks out the door. While he's gone, I just lie there. The windows are open, bringing a cool breeze into the room that feels pretty good on my face. I don't hear anything and I think it's really strange until I remember it's a weekday. But still, I can't remember the neighborhood ever being this quiet. Usually you'd hear something, somebody's car stereo with so much bass you can feel it in your insides, or a bunch of kids hanging out on the street because they're cutting school or something.

Marcus comes back in and I sit up a little. "Why weren't you at the funeral?" I ask him.

He shrugs, looking like he's going to walk right on by me. "Why aren't you still there?"

"I left," I said.

He just stands there a second, looking at me, and I get this sort of uncomfortable feeling, like I don't really know what to say to him. But it's a different feeling, different than I've ever felt around him before. I'm not afraid of him, or in awe, or nervous, or anything like that. I just don't know what to say.

I think he feels the same way, too, because he just goes back downstairs. For some reason, I decide to follow him.

He's standing in front of the closet with his back to me, but it doesn't look like he's going through it. He just stands there, daydreaming or something. The room's tiny, with barely enough space for the bed and the dresser. What little floor space there is, is almost covered with boxes. I think this is where Mom keeps all the Christmas stuff now because I see a box with tinsel sticking out of it.

Marcus doesn't seem to hear me come in. I push a box to the side and sit on the edge of the bed, watching him stare into the closet. All I can see are frilly-looking dresses and blouses and stuff. I guess Mom keeps some of the girls' stuff down here, too.

"I didn't know you still had stuff in there," I say, mainly to get his attention.

I see Marcus's head fall a little bit, and I wonder what kind of expression he has on his face.

But when he turns around, he looks as impassive as always. "I was just wondering if it was worth pushing all this shit aside to see if I still have anything else back there."

"You leaving town or something?"

Marcus shrugs. "Why do you ask that?"

"I don't know," I say. "It just looks like you're about to split or something."

"I might," he says. "I don't know yet. Depends on what I feel like doing."

"That simple?"

"Day by day," Marcus turns back to the closet. "Only way to live, man."

I look at the closet and see something bright green on the top shelf. "What's that up there?"

"What're you talking about?" Marcus asks.

I point to where I'm looking. "That green thing."

Marcus reaches up into the closet and pulls down this green plastic thing. He turns it over in his hands a few times, like he's trying to figure out what it is. It's only about a foot and a half long, real wide on one end and narrow on the other. "Little Slugger," Marcus reads on the side of it, and then he laughs.

"That's a baseball bat?" I ask. It's the weirdest-looking baseball bat I've ever seen.

"I used to bop you upside the head with this thing," Marcus says, still grinning. "Remember that?"

I think for a minute, then shake my head. I don't have many memories of being a little kid.

"And then you'd go crying to Mom, and she'd tell you to hit me back next time I hit you," Marcus goes on.

"How old was I?" I ask.

Marcus shrugs. "Two or three. Something like that."

"You remember being that little?" I ask.

"Yeah. Then one day I hit you and you grabbed the bat and hit me back. Almost knocked me out." He laughs. "Then I went crying to Mom." He grins at the bat and something looks weird about him. It takes me a while to realize that he almost looks happy.

Then he throws the bat into the closet and shuts the door. I just watch him as he moves over to the dresser, like he's forgotten all about the bat. I start wondering, who is he? Then I wonder if I'll ever have a chance to find out.

"Doesn't it bug you at all?" I ask.

Marcus turns to look at me. "What?"

"Tommy," I say, looking at him closely. "I mean, you liked him, didn't you?"

He shrugs. "Sure, I liked him."

"So doesn't it—" I stop because he's still looking at me like he doesn't know what I'm talking about. But he has to know, doesn't he? I try another tactic. "Do you know who did it?"

Marcus laughs a little, like he knows what I'm getting at and he knows better. "What do you want me to say, man?"

"I wanna know what you're gonna do," I say, looking right at him.

Marcus shakes his head. "What, you think I'm gonna act like Rambo or some shit like that? Man, you've been watching too many movies."

"So you're not gonna do nothing to whoever did this to Tommy," I say.

Marcus looks at me sort of quizzically. "I'll bet I know somebody who feels pretty damn guilty right now."

I let my head drop.

"I feel sorry for the guy, I really do," Marcus says.

That surprises the hell out of me. "You feel sorry for Zeke?"

"Sure," Marcus says, heading out the door and up the stairs. He keeps talking like he knows I'm following him, which I am. "I mean, he didn't exactly win his crusade, now did he?" But there's something mocking about Marcus's voice that tells me he doesn't really give a damn about Ezekiel, and that makes me feel bad. I wonder why, and then I realize that I'd stupidly thought I had reached some kind of new level with Marcus. I had thought he was really talking to me.

I cross the living room to sit on the couch as he moves to the door with a box. "What if it's you next time?"

Marcus stops and turns around. "If somebody off me, I ain't gonna know anyway. All the shit you see, you let that eat you up and you go crazy, like Zeke. That kid's half crazy already."

"So what do you know about Zeke, since you know so much about everything else?"

Marcus shakes his head, still grinning in that crooked way of his. I must sound stupid. "Now I never said that. But Zeke, that kid lets everything going down around him eat him alive. Don't take no rocket scientist to see that. And even if Tommy had listened to him, that wouldn't have been enough. The kid wanted to take on the whole world by himself, and he's the one who ended up broken down."

I remember the reverend wondering if Ezekiel was born in the wrong century, and the picture of Ezekiel lying there in the hospital comes back to me again. I guess I can't get that picture out of my head at all.

Marcus comes to sit on the couch next to me, leaning back and stretching his legs in front of him. "Rage will keep you warm for a little while," he goes on. "Somebody shoots your homie, you shoot him, that'll keep you going for a while. But then, what happens when you can't take it anymore, huh? You start trying to take out your shit on the peckerwoods. Then, when they break you down, the shit all breaks down and then what?"

"So what're you supposed to do, huh? How much're you supposed to take?"

Marcus doesn't answer that. I keep looking at him, remembering that almost businesslike expression on his face when he was slamming Ezekiel's head into the ground, like he was intent on killing him. The same look he had on his face when he was slamming my head on the ground in the backyard. Like it was just something he had to do. No more, no less. And that same old edgy feeling comes back. Before I know it, I'm all tensed up again, like I'm wondering what his next move's going to be.

Marcus raises his eyebrows. "You're still staring at me, man."

I take a deep breath, remembering how I felt when Leandrea asked me if Marcus had shot Ezekiel. "Could you kill somebody?"

Marcus shrugs. "Anybody can kill somebody. That's all circumstance."

"Could you kill me?"

Marcus laughs. "What kind of question is that?"

"I'm serious. Could you kill me? Or Mom or Gerald or Zeke or Reverend Washington? Could you do it?"

"Man—"

I feel myself growing impatient, and that edgy feeling turns into something else. "I mean, right now. You say you don't give a shit about nothing. Could you do it? I wanna know!"

For the first time, Marcus looks a little sad, even though he keeps on smiling. "Nah, man, I never said that. You said that."

I keep staring him down. "But you, you don't think about nobody, do you."

Marcus thinks for a minute, then shakes his head. "Well, then I'd have to hate people." He gets up and heads toward the door. "See you 'round, man," he says before he walks out.

I just sit there looking after him, not knowing what to think. I remember how I couldn't understand how Ezekiel could look Marcus in the face and not be afraid, even just a little. But this time, I wasn't afraid of him. And I know I'll never be afraid of him again.

I go upstairs to my room and shut the door; and then I flop down on my bed. I want to shut my eyes and try to sleep, but I keep thinking about what the reverend said at the funeral. Somehow, some way, I have to make my peace, not just with Tommy being dead, but with all of it, with everything that's happened. I just don't have any idea how to do that.

I wonder when I'll ever see Marcus again, if I ever see him again. I don't know why that thought suddenly comes to my head. I know he's got enemies. I know there are people out there who would shoot him in a minute. And he's got to know that, too; how could he not know that? I wonder if he thinks about it, what it makes him do. I wonder if he wakes up imagining that he's going to get his head blown off that day. Maybe that's why he is the way he is.

For a second, I even wonder what I would feel like if it had been Marcus who died instead of Tommy. It's almost like there's something dead about Marcus already. It's in his eyes. He expects nothing, feels nothing, looks forward to nothing. It's funny—I used to envy the way he never lets anything bother him. Like our dad. But now I think I'd rather be dead myself than be him.

Chapter 16

I MUST'VE FALLEN ASLEEP BECAUSE THE NEXT THING I know, I hear a loud banging on my door, and then Gerald comes bursting in. "Goddamn, this room stinks!" he exclaims, slamming the door behind him.

I continue to lie there, but I start to get annoyed. What the hell does he want, anyway?

"Why didn't you come to the cemetery?" Gerald asks.

I roll over and rub my eyes, but I don't answer.

I hear the bed shift with his weight as he sits down next to me. "Have you been lying up here in bed all day?"

"Don't you got something to do?" I grumble, sitting up.

He puts a hand on my shoulder, which I shake off quickly. I don't want anybody touching me. "Why're you shut up like this, anyway?"

"What do you want?" I ask, getting annoyed.

Gerald takes a deep breath, like he's about to start lecturing me. "Look, I know this's been a hard day for all of us. And I know something's up with you and Zeke, 'cause you all didn't say two words to each other at the church. But you can't just lie up here shut off from the world."

"Are you finished?" I snap.

"Mom wants to know where you are," Gerald says. "I figured you were here."

I lie down again and shut my eyes. "Where is everybody?"

"Having dinner at Uncle Earl's," Gerald says. "I guess Aunt Lorraine's gonna stay there a while. You know, till she gets back on her feet."

I nod.

"Zeke asked about you."

I open my eyes and look at Gerald. "Yeah?"

Gerald nods. "He doesn't look too good. I think he's taking it real hard." Gerald clasps his hands together and stares at the floor. "In fact, I think it'd be a good idea if you went over to talk to him. Whatever's going on between the two of you, you should just let it go. It's not important."

I sigh, not wanting to think about Ezekiel yet.

But Gerald gets this exasperated look on his face as he turns to face me, like he thinks I'm still really pissed off or something. "What the hell's the matter with you, huh?" he exclaims. "I come in here to check on you, see if you're okay, and you gotta be all of that?"

I sit there wondering if it's worth the effort to try to defend myself.

"You're such a kid, you know that?" he goes on. "Something's up with you and you gotta sit in your room like a goddamn two-year-old and pout about it?"

"Is that what you think I'm doing?" I ask finally. I wish he'd just leave because I'm sick of hearing his voice.

"That's what it looks like to me!" Gerald snaps, looking really pissed off. "What do I gotta do, huh? Knock some sense into you?"

I throw myself back on the bed. "You don't know shit."

"What're you talking about?" Gerald says, standing up. He comes to stand right over me.

"You come in here all hysterical and shit and you don't even know what's up," I say, turning on my side so I'm facing the wall.

Then I feel a hard jerk on my arm, and the next thing I know, I'm on my feet, looking up into Gerald's face. He's wrenching my arm, and it takes everything in me not to wince. "We don't got time for this," Gerald says. "We gotta go be with the family. We need to be with the family."

I grit my teeth and wrench myself away from him, and we stand face-to-face. "Go tell Mom that I wanna be by myself," I say. "I just need to be by myself for a while."

"Why're you acting like this, huh?" Gerald exclaims. "What is up with you?"

I look at him standing there huffing and puffing, and I sit down. "Y'know, if I'm pissed off now, it's because of you."

Gerald frowns. "What?"

"I mean, I was all right till you got here. Just lying here, chilling."

Gerald sits down next to me, but he doesn't say anything.

"Marcus might be leaving town," I say.

"How do you know that?" Gerald asks.

"He was here when I got back." I lie down again, and for some reason, I start feeling really calm.

Gerald clasps his hands together again. "What was he doing here?"

"Picking up some stuff," I say. "I guess he still had some stuff here. But he took it all with him."

"Did he take off with anything else?" Gerald snaps.

"I don't think so." That hadn't really occurred to me at all. I guess he could have. But then again, I can't think of anything here that he'd really want, or that he couldn't get for himself.

I expect Gerald to put on that uppity, pissed-off look of his and take another crack at Marcus, but he doesn't. He gets up and starts pacing back and forth from the window to the door, which for him is only about four steps, making me as uncomfortable as hell. "You know, sometimes I feel like everything's just falling apart. We can't depend on Dad for shit—" He stops talking and he looks sad. I can see how much Dad really hurts him.

"Why do you bother?" I ask.

"What?"

"About Dad, you know?"

"He's still my dad, you know?" Gerald says. "I wanna know who he is. If you don't got your family, you don't got nothing."

I don't say anything to that little piece of irony, and we just sit there a minute without saying anything.

"Does he know about Tommy?" I finally ask.

"I don't think so," Gerald mutters. "I haven't been by to see him."

"You better get over to the reverend's," I say.

"You coming?" he asks.

I shake my head. "Nah."

He looks sort of discouraged, so I say, "I'm gonna go for a walk or something. Tell everybody—well, tell them I can't make it."

Gerald nods and walks out without saying anything else.

I want to get out of the house; I do know that. I just don't want to be around a lot of people. I lean over to pull off the slacks I'm wearing and put on a pair of jeans instead. Then I take off the dress shirt and put on a T-shirt and tie up my shoes. I don't know where I'm going to go, or what I'm going to do. I can't make a big production about it, like I've all of a sudden found some answer to the meaning of life or anything like that. I just get up. I'm not pissed off about anything or worried or upset or anything like that. I've been through all of that already, and now I'm just here.

It's still sunny outside. The streets have come alive now. I can hear screaming kids and screaming parents and bass stereos, as usual. I start walking, past all the little kids running bags of grass and sugar back and forth across the street, until I'm standing on the court, that old familiar place where me and the fellas always hung out. But that feels like a lifetime ago. A bunch of guys play three-on-three on one of the courts, laughing and talking trash to each other, and I just stand there a second, watching them. For some reason I feel really old. I'm not exactly sure why, because the guys look around my age, and it's not like I'm not going to hang out here with Ezekiel and Willy and Lavias anymore, or anything like that. I guess what's different now is me. I can't just be some silent spectator anymore. I can't hide inside myself anymore, if that makes any sense. Too much has happened for me to do that now. Before, I always noticed things, saw things, then put it all in the back of my head, letting it all eat at me. And then I'd try to shut it all out and pretend it wasn't there. I never let myself really think about everyone I know: my dad, Ezekiel, Marcus, Gerald, Reverend Washington, and what they all mean to me. I guess I was always mad because there wasn't one person I could really look up to who could teach me things, show me how to be a man. I never let myself really think about things because I was afraid how alone I would feel when I realized that there was nobody really there.

I walk back into my neighborhood, over to the side where my father lives. And soon I'm in front of his house. I stand there for a second, looking at the peeling paint, the unkempt yard. I see that shiny new Saturn of his in the driveway. Maybe he took the day off work or something. I get this sudden urge to talk to him. I think of the last time I was here, how I couldn't really say anything to him because I was afraid I'd break down or something or that he'd be able to see how much he's hurt me. But I can't be worried about stuff like that now. I think about what Gerald said about getting to know the guy, and I feel this rush of words bombarding my head. And it isn't even about wanting to know him. I want him to know me. I want him to know what I think of him. I want him to know exactly why I never come around to see him and how I wish he'd just be real with me, instead of pretending he's always been there for us when he hasn't been. I'm going to tell him exactly what I think he is, and it's not going to make me feel worn out, like I did when I told off Ezekiel, or upset, like I felt when I told off Marcus. It's going to make me feel like a man instead of like a kid. The next thing I know, I'm banging on the door like I'm trying to break it down or something.

The door opens and I don't see anything. Then I look down and see one of his little girls looking up at me with a dirty face and big brown eyes. "Your dad here?" I ask her.

"No."

"Where is he?"

The kid stands there looking at me, leaning against the door. "I dunno."

"When did he leave?"

"Couple days ago."

"Couple of days ago?" I say and scratch my head. "But isn't that his car out there?"

The girl glances toward the driveway. "That's Mommy's car," she says. "She says Daddy couldn't take it with him."

I feel myself frowning. "Know when he'll be back?"

Her eyes get all serious-looking. "Mommy says he's not coming back."

I stand there for a second, staring at the ground. Then I chuckle. Or maybe it's a sob; I don't know, but I swallow it down, mumble something, and turn from the door, back to the street.

I walk up the street in a daze, my throat dry. I should have asked the kid for a glass of water or something, but I keep walking, not knowing where the hell I'm going. So he left. Son of a bitch. That rush of words to my head from a minute ago, it just dissolves. Dissolves into nothing. I can't even feel angry about it. There's nothing to be angry about. I sort of laugh again. So he left. What the hell's new? As I keep walking, I start to feel really sorry for Gerald. It's going to tear him up when he finds out. But me, I don't really know what I'm feeling yet. Even though I always got annoyed at Gerald for trying to spend time with the guy and stuff, I guess all along I wanted the same thing Gerald did. I just wanted a dad.

As I walk home, I realize that my father will call in a couple of months like he always does to tell us where he is now, what he's doing, who he's with, to talk and laugh like we're all the best of friends. I wonder what I'll do when he calls, if I'll have that same frustrated-hurt-angry feeling I usually have when I think about it. Maybe a week ago I would have felt like that, but now I don't know. I'm somewhere else now. Someplace I can't go back on.

I can't think of anywhere else to go, so I walk home. I go to the living room and sit there the rest of the afternoon watching TV, or staring at the TV really, until my mom gets home from the reverend's. When I hear her come in, I'm on my feet, following her upstairs to her room.

"Todd?" She looks surprised to see me as she kicks off her shoes. "We all missed you."

I don't say anything. I just sit next to her on the bed and put my head in her lap. I don't even know what to say, or how to say it. But she seems to get it. She just sits there stroking my head, not saying anything. And as I lie there, I think there's something about women that makes them strong. Leandrea showed me that really, just by the way she could open herself up to me without being afraid what I'd think, while I always try to shut everything out and then probably look the fool because everything you feel always comes out anyway. Ezekiel showed me that, how everything in you can just explode in ways you don't mean it to. Then again, I didn't need Ezekiel to show me that. I guess it's easier to see things in other people than it is to see things in yourself.

Still, I feel sad as I sit there, feeling the slow regularity of my mother's breathing. I think of how my mom cries sometimes when she thinks nobody's looking. How much it bugs me to see her because then I'd have to think about everything that's going on with her. I can't remember the last time I saw her do something for herself, but then again, I wouldn't even know what she would want for herself if she could get it. I guess it's too bad that it took Leandrea for me to start thinking about my mom. But I feel good anyway, because I can come to her and just let her hold me; and she will, without asking me why I'm here or anything when I hardly ever speak to her. As I lie there, I feel safe, the way I used to feel when I would come crying to her as a little kid. And I can't believe it's taken me all this time to remember how good that felt.

Chapter 17

I'M SITTING AROUND THE HOUSE WATCHING TV THE NEXT afternoon when I hear the doorbell. I go to open the door, wondering who'd be coming by in the middle of the day, and I see Leandrea standing there.

I blink a few times when I see her because she looks different to me. It takes me a second to realize she's cut off all her hair real short, so it curls around her ears.

"How're you doing?" she asks.

"All right," I say quickly, standing aside so that she can come in. "What brings you by?"

Leandrea shrugs. "I haven't seen you in a while. I wanted to know how you were doing." She looks sort of nervous. "I saw Willy at school today, and he told me where you live."

I nod, not really knowing what to say, either. I'm glad to see her, I know that. I guess I'm just sort of overwhelmed.

"Um, I brought by the English assignment," she says quickly, reaching into her book bag. "I told Ms. Anders why you weren't in class and stuff. Anyway, we have to write an essay on Macbeth. Here are the topics."

"Thanks," I say, taking the paper she hands to me. But I don't look at it. "Wanna come upstairs?" I lead her up to my room because my sisters are downstairs in the kitchen.

Leandrea wanders in, stepping over a pile of clothes on the floor to sit on a chair across from my bed. I get sort of embarrassed that she's here, not really because my room's a mess, but it's always weird to have people in your room for the first time because they're seeing a part of you that they haven't seen before. My room looks stark with its bare, dingy walls, and it has my own funky smell from my dirty clothes on the floor. I go to open a window and shove the clothes under the bed.

"So really, Todd, how are you doing?" she asks.

I sit on the bed. "All right, I guess."

"The funeral was nice."

That surprises me. "I didn't see you there."

"You and Ezekiel were with your families and I didn't want to bother you," she says. "I sat with Lavias. He didn't tell you?"

"Haven't seen him," I say.

"Oh," she says.

"Why'd you cut your hair?"

Leandrea laughs a little and reaches up to touch her hair. "You like it?"

I cock my head and look at her from the side. It makes her look younger and her eyes look bigger, I think, but she still looks good. "Yeah, it's all right."

"Well, I hate it," she says. "I think I look like an elf."

"So why'd you do it?"

"I got into a fight with my dad." Leandrea touches her hair again; then her eyes fall to the floor. "I told him I was only going to apply to all-black colleges next year and he blew up. He said, 'Those kinds of schools give you a false sense of what the world is like, and you have to live in the real world.' And then I said something like 'You just want me to pretend I'm white.' I swear, sometimes he acts like the fact that I'm light-skinned and have long hair is the most important thing about me. So I went up in the bathroom and took the scissors to my hair. He loves my hair. Always has. Never let me cut it or anything. So I come downstairs with my hair all short, and he about has a heart attack. Tells me I don't appreciate anything he's trying to do for me. Then Mom takes me off to the salon so they can do a better job."

Leandrea looks up at me now. "But you know, he still won. He still won because I hate it. I hate this haircut."

"It doesn't look bad," I say.

She shrugs. "But that's not even the point, really. I did it because of him, not because I wanted short hair. I did it just to piss him off. It makes me wonder if I can really do anything for myself." She sighs abruptly. "I didn't mean to get into all of that."

"No, it's all right," I say.

She nods, still looking sort of uncomfortable. "How's Ezekiel?"

I shrug. "I haven't really talked to him, either."

"Something happened between you guys, right?" she says seriously.

I shrug again, not really knowing what to say.

"It's okay; you don't have to talk about it," she says. "I know you guys'll work it out, anyway."

"Yeah," I say, sort of vaguely.

"You know, it's funny how you and Ezekiel are so different," she goes on. "I mean, you two have such different ways of looking at things and doing things, but you can still hang out and be really close."

I start thinking about that.

Leandrea sighs. "I've never had friends like that. I guess girls are different that way. Maybe we have to have more things in common than guys do, or maybe we're more competitive about everything."

We both fall silent for a minute, wrapped up in our own thoughts, I guess. I see her looking at me in a really funny way, like she's sad about something. I haven't really thought about her a lot lately because so many other things were going on, but as I sit there looking at her, it all comes back to me. Just looking at her does something to me. I sort of wish she hadn't come. Maybe I was better off not thinking about her.

Then she gets up and comes to sit on the bed next to me. She's still wearing that sad look on her face. "You've been so nice to me," she says so softly I can barely hear her.

I sort of shrug. I mean, what can I say to that?

"You've listened to me, let me ramble on and on about everything," she goes on. "I feel like I can tell you anything. I've never had a friend like you before."

I know that's supposed to make me feel good, but it doesn't. Friend. That's all I am to her, all I can ever be to her. It makes me wonder how long it'll take before I'm okay with it, with just being her friend and nothing else.

"Are you okay?" she asks.

I must have a weird look on my face or something, so I lean back on my hands and try to play it off. "Have you seen Zeke?"

She shakes her head, sort of expressionless. So I guess they haven't made up or gotten back together or anything like that. Then I ask myself what difference that makes.

"You know, I can be so shallow," she says.

"What?"

"I made Zeke out to be this big hero. But you know, I don't know who he really is. I've been thinking about that, how I got all mad at him last Sunday for making me out like just some girl, but I did the same thing. I made him into something I wanted him to be."

"Everybody does stuff like that," I say.

"Do you?"

I get uncomfortable because I don't really know what she's getting at. I turn to look at her and I sort of wish I hadn't, because I get drawn into her all over again. I look right into those blue eyes of hers; then I look at her skin, all soft and smooth-looking. She's got a little mole right next to her left eye. I'm surprised I never noticed it before, as much as I've checked her out. She's got a zit on her cheek, almost next to her hairline so it's sort of out of sight. All I can think about is how I felt when I saw her at church that Sunday, looking like something out of a magazine or a movie, untouchable. And here she is now, her face so close to mine that all I'd have to do is move two inches or so and I'd be kissing her. I know it shows. It's got to be written all over my face, everything I'm feeling for her.

She gets this curious look on her face. "What do you think of me, Todd?"

I glance toward the window, playing off like something caught my attention. But then I just feel stupid. I'll bet she knows I'm fronting.

"Todd?" Her hand brushes against mine, but I take a deep breath to keep myself steady.

"What do you want me to say?" My voice sounds pissed off, but when I look at her again she doesn't seem upset or even embarrassed. She just looks at me.

"I don't gotta tell you you look good or nothing like that," I say—mumble, really. "And it's kinda weird, you being here—with me. I mean, I never thought you would be."

I expect her to look all sad again and give me one of those you're-a-nice-guy-but-no-thanks speeches, but she doesn't say anything. Instead, she shuts her eyes and sort of tilts her head and before I know it I'm kissing her. I can't tell you how it started, or who started it, or anything like that. All I know is that I've got my arms wrapped around her waist and then we're lying there on my bed. I don't even know what I'm thinking, if I'm doing any thinking at all. The whole world has turned into her. I kiss her all over her face, all over her neck, feel her legs wrapped tight around my hips, feel her tongue all warm and wet in my mouth. I bury my face in her neck and breathe deeply as she pins her hips down against mine. I'm going out of my mind. My jeans start feeling real tight and real uncomfortable and I feel a sweat break out on my forehead.

And then she sits up and moves away from me real quick, like somebody's walked in on us or something. She takes deep breaths, like she's trying to pull herself together. "I can't do this," she says, her shoulders heaving up and down.

I feel myself tense up. Did I do something? "O-okay—"

She shuts her eyes and shakes her head. "It's not you," she says, still sounding out of breath. "It's me."

I just nod. To tell you the truth, I'm getting scared.

"There's so much you don't know about me, Todd," she says. Her hair's sticking up, sort of messy-looking.

"Yeah?" I say, not knowing what she's getting at.

She takes another deep breath, smoothing down her hair. "You don't know anything about how I used to be, do you?"

I don't answer because I don't know what to say.

"I don't exactly have a great reputation," she says. "I used to date a lot of white guys. It was like, I was dark enough so it could be all daring to go out with me, but I was light enough so it wasn't too big a deal, you know?"

I sit there sort of taken aback. "You don't gotta tell me this."

"Yeah, I do," she says and then she stops looking at me. "Because I've never had anybody look at me like you do and it scares me and it makes me feel incredible and I—I don't know if you'll still look at me like that if you really know about me."

"I don't know what you're getting at," I say.

"Have you ever done something wrong and known

it's been wrong, even when you're doing it, but you can't stop yourself?" Now she looks at me again, but her face is sort of guarded, the way it was when I first met her.

I shrug, getting this uncomfortable feeling. I don't want to hear anything else. I want us to just lie here and feel good about something.

"It's just so easy to do," she says.

I move toward her, wanting to kiss her again so that she doesn't have to talk.

Leandrea scoots away from me. "I knew how guys talked about me and stuff." She talks faster, like she's got to get something out. So I just listen.

"But those few moments I was with somebody, I'd feel so—" She stops a second; then she goes on. "I guess it was my screwed-up way of trying to feel like I fit in somewhere. Who knows, maybe all along I knew that I didn't. I always tried to play it off like I was the user, I was the one in control, but I wasn't. And then I'd get pissed off at myself for being so dumb, you know? And then, this semester, when I saw Ezekiel in class, saw the way he stood up for things, how he tried to make himself into what he wanted to be, I thought I wanted to be strong like he is. I wanted to be proud of myself. And I thought I could be that way with him.

"I don't know how he saw me. I think he just saw me as some girl who was into him. So I tried to be different.

I wanted to show him I wasn't just some girl. I wanted to show myself that, too. But no matter what I did, that's how he saw me. He was too into himself to see me any other way. And then—"

She looks at me now. Hard and deep. "I didn't tell you everything that happened Sunday."

I don't know if I want to hear any more.

"He came over all upset like I said," she says, speaking in a real low voice. "And I told you how I tried to talk to him about my dad, and how he wasn't really listening to me. And, I don't know." She stops and clears her throat. "I wanted him to know what I was thinking. I wanted him to know so much, but he just wasn't listening to me. And then I just gave up. I didn't care anymore and I just let it happen."

Huh? I think to myself. Let what happen? But she sits there looking at me so seriously and I see something in her eyes that looks like shame. "You slept with Zeke?" I exclaim.

"No." She shakes her head quickly. "No—almost. But what difference did it make, really? I was still just some dumb girl to him. It would have been so easy to, you know, but I don't know, it was just wrong. The whole thing felt wrong but there we were, totally getting together. That's when I threw him off."

I blink a couple of times, trying to picture them together, getting that jealous, half-crazy feeling I had up at the cabin, and then I catch her face and see her looking sad and I just—I don't know what to think.

"I was so mad at myself," she says. "I think he knew I was mad at myself. I think he might've tried to say he was sorry about it or something if I had let him, but you see? He wasn't the one who blew it. I did. And now, what do I do?" She shakes her head and laughs. "I start getting together with his best friend. I am such a bitch!"

I don't know what to say.

She looks at me sort of defiantly. "I'll bet you don't think I'm so great now, do you?"

I think for a minute, think about everything she's said. And the more I look at her, the simpler it all gets. She's somebody who's done things wrong, just like I have. The more I look at her, the more I realize that I'm in love with her. Plain and simple. But I don't really know how to say that. I try to think of something to say that'll tell her that without using those words exactly, but everything I think of just sounds all hokey. "Hey, Leandrea."

She doesn't say anything.

"I hope this doesn't sound dumb or nothing, but—"

Her expression doesn't change. "But what?"

"I—" I begin, trying to choose my words carefully. Then I just give up. "I mean—I don't hate you or nothing."

She looks like she's trying to put everything together

or something. When she looks up again, she smiles at me and her eyes are sort of shiny. I know that she gets it.

"I should get going," she says softly.

Before I know it, my hand moves over to hers. "You have to go right now?"

She nods, and if I'm right, she looks like she doesn't want to leave either. "I told my mom I'd meet her for coffee."

"Can you come back afterward?" I ask, squeezing her hand a little.

"I don't know when it would be," she says. "Mom might want to take me shopping or something."

I shrug. "I'll be here."

She smiles. "Then I'll come back. Will you walk me out?"

I lead her down the steps to the front door, and we stand there a minute. Then she leans over to kiss me. Her mouth is really soft, and it's enough to make me want to go back upstairs with her right now. "I'll come back," she says.

I watch her go out to her car and drive away.

Chapter 18

EZEKIEL COMES OVER LATE IN THE AFTERNOON.

I'd been sitting around all afternoon thinking about Leandrea, wondering when she would come by, but the first time the doorbell rang it was Willy and Lavias. We sat around my living room playing cards because it looked like it was about to rain and we didn't want to get stuck out on the court. Now I'm waiting for Leandrea while Lavias and Willy play each other at Blackjack. The doorbell rings again and I jump up to answer it. Ezekiel stands in the doorway.

I just stand there looking at him for a second. This is the first time I've really seen him since he got out of the hospital. His jeans are baggier, like he lost some weight, and he looks small to me for some reason, like he lost some of his height, too. Or maybe it's just the way he's standing shifty-eyed in the doorway, his hands in his jacket pockets, like he doesn't know what to say. He's not green anymore, but he's still sort of pale.

"Hey, man, whassup?" Lavias says as Ezekiel comes in.

"Join the game," Willy says, grinning.

Ezekiel comes in and sits on the couch. "What're you playing?"

"Blackjack. That fool's winning 'cause he cheats," Willy says.

"Man, you say that, but you're losing!" Lavias shoots back.

Ezekiel grins a little, but he looks tired. Not sleepy-tired, but worn-out-tired. I sit there looking at him for a minute, not really knowing what to say. From the way he's acting, I can tell he doesn't really know what to say to me either.

Lavias puts down another twenty-one and Willy throws his cards on the table. "Aw, man, you do cheat!"

Lavias shrugs, still grinning. "Ain't my fault you're lousy!"

Ezekiel stands up. "Yo, Todd, got a minute?"

I walk out to the front porch, and he follows me. We both sit down, looking out on the street. The sky's all purple and black, like a storm's about to bust any minute. We just sit there for a second, not really looking at each other, not saying anything.

"Know what I kept seeing over and over when I was in the hospital?" Ezekiel says out of nowhere. I look at him and see him looking up at the sky. His face is sort of blank. Reserved, like there's a lot going on inside that he doesn't want to show.

"What?"

"A house." He keeps looking out, like he's talking to himself more than he's talking to me. "A house that don't got no doors or windows. Just walls and a roof. And I'm inside it, but nobody knows I'm in there. And the house, it's burning down and I can't tell anybody I'm in there and I can't do nothing to get out. I just smell the smoke, start choking on it, feel the heat from the flames even though the fire hasn't gotten to me yet, and I'm scared as shit 'cause there ain't nothing I can do about it. No way out."

I sit there and nod. I don't look at him and he doesn't look at me. Both of us keep looking ahead at the street. Both of us fall silent as we sit there. I hear the first break of thunder and look up, waiting for the downpour.

"Leandrea's gonna be here soon," I say for no reason. Or maybe there is a reason. Maybe I want to see how he'll react.

He doesn't do anything for a minute. "I could have figured that."

"It ain't about you, either," I say, still not looking at him. Both of our voices are flat and I have to think, what is it that I'm feeling about this guy? I don't hate him; I know that, at least. All I have inside is a deep sense of calm. "It's about me and her."

"Yeah, I know," he says, his voice flat as mine. "That's what I meant."

"You mean you don't care or nothing?"

I hear him sigh again. This time I turn to look at him. I want to see his face. He's looking at the ground, looking at his hands, but he doesn't look mad or anything. "Nah."

I turn out to the street again. "Why not?" Maybe I'm trying to pick a fight with him, I don't know.

"I dunno," he says. "Anyways, I can't be thinking about that too much anyway. I got other things to be thinking about—"

I just nod.

Ezekiel stares ahead of himself. "The reverend wants to send me somewhere this summer. Jamaica or the Dominican Republic or something like that. Some church thing or another. He thinks it'll be good for me. Get my head back together or something."

"You gonna go?"

"Nah. Got too much stuff to be figuring out here. I think I wanna start something up."

"Huh?" I say.

"At the church," he says. "Not Bible study or no shit like that. I already talked to the reverend about it. We're gonna set up a program, you know? So that maybe what happened—won't happen no more."

"That sounds like a good thing to do."

"Yeah." Ezekiel rubs his forehead. "Wanna help out with it?"

"Yeah, sure."

Ezekiel just nods, but he still looks sort of distant. I've never seen him this quiet before. "You seen Marcus around?"

"I saw him a couple days ago," I say. "I think he was about to split."

"Yeah?" Ezekiel says.

"He was taking all his stuff out of the house," I say. "I don't really know what's up with him."

"Did you talk to him?"

"The day I left you at the hospital, you know," I swallow, feeling sort of uncomfortable for bringing that up. "I came back here and Marcus was here and I got so pissed off, I took him on, you know?"

Ezekiel raises his eyebrows. "What happened?"

I chuckle a little. "I got my ass whupped, that's what happened."

A grin flickers at the corner of Ezekiel's mouth, too, but it goes away quickly. "I don't think he left town or nothing."

"Why do you say that?"

"Isaiah says he saw him yesterday in the park," Ezekiel says, then clears his throat. "See the paper this morning?"

I shake my head.

"Couple of guys got smoked last night. A couple of guys that were there, you know?" He looks at me. "Think Marcus did it?"

"I don't know," I say. "I don't know what's up with Marcus."

Ezekiel just nods again; he sits there with a look on his face that I can't read.

"Whassup?" I ask him.

"I miss my mom," he says.

I jolt a little because I never expected him to say that. I don't really know what to say in response.

"You know, I've always been so pissed off at her for dying, but then, lying up there in that hospital—I dunno—" He stares at the ground again.

For a moment I think of when Aunt Jessie died. I remember, I was with Zeke every day, just sitting there in his room with him, trying to get him to talk. I would read newspapers out loud, try to mess with him and stuff, but he just lay there on his bed staring into space with the same look on his face that he's wearing now. After a week he said something to me about UNLV basketball, but to my knowledge he's never spoken of his mother since. And I think of him carrying that around all this time, all that hurt, knowing he doesn't have anybody to go to when he feels like a little kid, and I feel really sorry for him.

"So you like the girl? Leandrea, I mean?" Ezekiel says.

"Yeah."

For a second there he gets his old self-righteous look on his face, and he sits up a little. "You know, she ain't—"

"She told me about a lot of stuff," I tell him so that he doesn't have to say anything else.

"She did?" Ezekiel frowns. "I hope she didn't try to say I did something to her or any shit like that, 'cause I didn't." He stops talking suddenly, like he knows that none of it really matters anymore. And I don't say anything in response.

He just shakes his head and sighs, and I see right there how much he really liked her, even though he didn't know how to show it. He shrugs and tries to laugh it off, but I see right through it. "You've got your mom, and now you've got Leandrea, too."

"But you've got your dad," I interrupt him. "Somebody who'll do anything for you."

Ezekiel sighs. "I guess."

"My dad left," I say, my voice flat. "He just up and walked out on his girlfriend and her kids. Who knows where he went."

Ezekiel shakes his head. "That's too bad, man."

I look at him for a second, surprised to hear him say that. A week ago he would have made some remark about what a shit my dad is, but now he looks genuinely sorry. I shrug. "He ain't never gonna be a father to me. I know that."

"It's a bitch, ain't it," Ezekiel says.

"I guess you just gotta learn to be happy with what you got."

Ezekiel nods slowly. "I guess." But he still looks sad in a way that makes me feel sad, too. Even more than that, I feel just how close we really are. It isn't even that we're cousins, or that I feel like I've known him even longer than I've known myself, but all that emptiness, the lack of direction. Ezekiel took it all outside of himself and put it into trying to save Tommy, while I just kept all of my feeling inside, seething in me. And I think, all that energy I put into being jealous of him, thinking I hated him, I could have put into trying to understand him, because to understand him would be to understand me in a lot of ways.

I turn to look at him, watch him staring out at nothing, seeing all of the pain he feels, and I wonder if he feels like a failure. And then, knowing what I know about him, I know he has to.

"You know, both those bullets were meant for me," he says.

"How do you know that?"

"I just do."

I shake my head, trying to think of something to tell him that isn't true. Because that's too much for anybody to be carrying around. "It wasn't your fault, man."

"Yeah, it was," he mutters, frowning.

"No, it wasn't," I say. "Tommy beat up that kid; those

guys might've gone looking for him, anyway. Let it go, man. Just let it go."

He turns to look at me, his black eyes wide and deep. "What if they'd killed me?"

I shudder. "Don't say that—"

"I mean it. What if it was me who died and not Tommy?" He keeps looking at me like he's expecting an answer, so I look straight ahead and think, allow myself to visualize that possibility, and I go cold inside. Cold and dead.

I turn to look him straight in the eye. "Man, I don't know what I'd do." He continues to look at me, so I sigh and shake my head. "If you died . . . shoot, they'd have to bury me, too."

Ezekiel grins at that. I just clap him on the shoulder, not knowing what else to say to him, but he seems to get it.

Leandrea drives up and parks the Cabriolet behind Gerald's truck. I can't help but grin as I watch her come out, step toward me. I like her hair short, even if she doesn't. It really isn't all that flattering, but it makes her look more real somehow. She stops when she sees me with Ezekiel but then walks to us sort of stiffly. "Hi, Todd. Hi, Ezekiel," she says, sounding stiff as well.

Ezekiel nods, looks away; then he jumps to his feet. "I should get going. I've got some stuff to do for the reverend."

"I'll come by later," I tell him.

He nods and starts to walk away.

"Yo, Zeke," I call out to him.

He stops and turns around.

"The house—"

"What house?"

"It don't gotta burn you down, man."

He looks at me kind of weirdly, then turns around to walk up the street.

Leandrea and I watch him leave, and when he's gone, I slide down a step so that I'm sitting beside her. I put an arm around her shoulder, and she leans against me.

"What were you talking about?" she asks.

I don't answer. I keep my eyes on the road long after Ezekiel's gone.

"I really feel bad." She sighs. "I don't want to come between you guys."

"You won't," I tell her.

She doesn't say anything, but she still looks worried. I tighten my arm around her and kiss the side of her face, to let her know that everything's going to be all right. Maybe not the same way it used to be, but all right just the same.

Another peal of thunder shakes the sky, and Leandrea jumps a little. "Let's go inside."

But I continue to sit there, happy where I am, getting this sense of comfort from the thunder, like it's talking to me, telling me that everything's going to be all right with me and Ezekiel. But most of all I listen to myself, feeling something warm inside of me as I sit there with my arms around Leandrea. It's a feeling that tells me I can face anything and that I don't need to look to anyone else to find the answers to questions inside of me. I sit there with Leandrea wishing I could hold on to this moment forever, hearing the thunder and seeing the lightning split the sky. And I keep hearing those words I told Ezekiel in my mind. It don't gotta burn you down. It don't gotta burn you down. It don't gotta burn you down.

Lorri Hewett was born in Virginia and raised in Colorado. She loved reading as a young girl and began her writing career early, completing nine novels by the time she went to college.

Ms. Hewett wrote *Soulfire* while she was an undergraduate at Emory University in Atlanta, Georgia. It draws upon her own experiences and those of many of her friends at their ethnically mixed Denver-area high school.

Recently Ms. Hewett completed a graduate fellowship in English literature at St. Andrews University, Scotland. Her second novel, *Unlikely Ties*, will be published by Dutton in 1998.